SPACE MARINE
L E G E N D S

SHRIKE

GEORGE MANN

BLACK LIBRARY

To all my friends at GW past and present – with thanks.

A BLACK LIBRARY PUBLICATION

Shrike first published in 2016.
This edition published in Great Britain in 2017 by
Black Library,
Games Workshop Ltd.,
Willow Road,
Nottingham, NG7 2WS, UK.

10 9 8 7 6 5 4 3 2 1

Produced by Games Workshop in Nottingham.
Cover illustration by Akim Kaliberda.

See Black Library on the internet at

blacklibrary.com

Find out more about Games Workshop
and the world of Warhammer 40,000 at

games-workshop.com

Printed and bound in China

It is the 41st millennium. For more than a hundred centuries the Emperor has sat immobile on the Golden Throne of Earth. He is the master of mankind by the will of the gods, and master of a million worlds by the might of his inexhaustible armies. He is a rotting carcass writhing invisibly with power from the Dark Age of Technology. He is the Carrion Lord of the Imperium for whom a thousand souls are sacrificed every day, so that he may never truly die.

Yet even in his deathless state, the Emperor continues his eternal vigilance. Mighty battlefleets cross the daemon-infested miasma of the warp, the only route between distant stars, their way lit by the Astronomican, the psychic manifestation of the Emperor's will. Vast armies give battle in His name on uncounted worlds. Greatest amongst his soldiers are the Adeptus Astartes, the Space Marines, bioengineered super-warriors. Their comrades in arms are legion: the Astra Militarum and countless planetary defence forces, the ever-vigilant Inquisition and the tech-priests of the Adeptus Mechanicus to name only a few. But for all their multitudes, they are barely enough to hold off the ever-present threat from aliens, heretics, mutants – and worse.

To be a man in such times is to be one amongst untold billions. It is to live in the cruellest and most bloody regime imaginable. These are the tales of those times. Forget the power of technology and science, for so much has been forgotten, never to be re-learned. Forget the promise of progress and understanding, for in the grim dark future there is only war. There is no peace amongst the stars, only an eternity of carnage and slaughter, and the laughter of thirsting gods.

PART ONE

VETERAN

The forest was all. The forest was everything.

Shrike crouched behind the tangled bough of an immense bolas tree, carefully measuring every breath, every rustle or creak of movement. Sunlight pierced the canopy high above, dappled shafts questing through the lattice of branches to pick out an overturned stump here, a bundle of exposed roots there. To Shrike, the forest had taken on an eerie, ghostly quality, as if the trees themselves were holding their breath, anticipating what might come next.

It had been three hours since he'd moved, and even the bolas tree had relaxed in his presence; its roots had once again begun to worm their way through the topsoil, digging for nutritious beetles. Birds and howler feeks darted amongst its upper branches, and Shrike had become so attuned to the ambient noise that to him every twitch of a wing, every scratch of a claw, sounded like a thunder-clap. Even his own pulse, wilfully slowed to a sluggish, occasional thud, was like an explosive charge detonating inside his head.

He blinked, and his lids scraped across the dry, glassy surfaces of his eyes. He was ready, waiting for his moment to pounce.

He wore nothing but a light loincloth, his pale, thewed torso exposed to the elements. He'd shed his clothing the moment he'd entered the forest, aware of how it hindered his movement, how the rustle of fabric alerted those around him. The last thing he needed was to draw attention. He knew all too well that there were predators in the forest.

Today, he was one of them.

Shrike allowed another breath to whistle out between his teeth. He eyed the fallen branch, no more than a few feet away. It rested on the mulch of the forest floor where it had fallen, jutting from amongst the decaying leaves like the felled antlers of some gigantic beast. Moss had begun to creep up the sides of it, slowly subsuming it, pulling it back down into the earth. Nature moved swiftly on Kiavahr, always anxious to reclaim its own. Soon one of the sleek Kiavahran ravens would land here, searching amongst the foliage for grubs, and then he would make his move.

That was the reason he was here: to prove his worth, to claim a raven as his own.

Success was essential. He had allowed himself no other option. To succeed today was to become one of the Raven Guard, the Emperor's champions, the black-clad warriors from the sky – to sail out amongst the stars, bringing redemption to the many worlds of the Imperium of Man. Even the thought of it made Shrike's pulse quicken, and he quashed his rising sense of anticipation.

All he had to do was catch a raven and take its skull as his personal totem, his *corvia*. That was all – the final challenge, the last stage of his initiation. After so many trials, both physical and mental, this was the moment that truly mattered.

It sounded such a simple task: a single, solitary bird, from a forest of thousands.

He'd lived alongside the ravens his entire life, throwing them crumbs from his table, whistling along to their birdsong as he traipsed through the forest as a boy. To Shrike, they'd been a constant presence, as familiar to him as his own shadow.

Only now, he had to catch one and wring its neck. More than that, he had to do it with his bare hands.

Shrike steadied his nerves. He had to remain focused, to stop his mind from drifting.

The forest was all. The forest was everything.

This was his mantra, the means by which he banished all unwelcome thoughts. He repeated it, rolling it over in his head. To fail now would be to remain here, on Kiavahr, for the rest of his existence. To never fulfil his potential and take to the stars.

He was one of many aspirants, and he knew that only a handful of them would succeed. He'd watched some of the brightest and best of his clan fall by the wayside during the physical trials that preceded the hunt, and as he'd watched them skulking back to their arboreal domes, he had vowed never to join them in their regret and dismay. He was made for the stars. He was made for war. He knew this with a certainty that he had never known anything else before. Nothing would stand in his way.

Two of his clan brothers were close by. He could sense them, lurking amongst the bolas trees in search of their own prey, their own path to glory. They, too, had been hand picked from their clan by the Space Marines, deemed worthy to test their mettle against the trials and earn their place as initiates in the order.

They were close to the sacred burial site of the Space Marines, here, a part of the forest forbidden to mere younglings such as Shrike, Corus and Kadus. It hadn't stopped them, however, imagining the training exercises taking place inside. They'd even crept close on one occasion, scaling the nearby bolas trees to peer in over the compound walls, but had been able to discern nothing amongst the inky shadows inside.

This was where the successful initiates would be taken for their training, before going on to Deliverance, the moon that served as the Chapter's fortress base. Shrike had often stared up at that glimmering orb, awed by how distant it seemed. Today, it seemed a little closer, almost within reach.

He'd seen what became of the initiates, the changes wrought on their physique and attitude – how they went in as boys and came out as... something *else* – but the notion didn't frighten him. Indeed, he relished the prospect. He longed to become more than he was, to *belong*. He longed to defend his home and the homes of others oppressed by the alien menace, to expand his horizons beyond the forest and know the secrets of the universe.

Shrike breathed. He closed his eyes, banishing all thoughts of Corus and Kadus, and the ebon-armoured warriors in the compound.

When he opened them again, a raven was perched upon the fallen branch. He felt his hand trembling. This was his chance, the moment he'd been waiting for – not for three hours, but for his entire life.

The bird had its back to him, preening its feathers with its beak. He took a moment to admire its beauty. That's what the instructors had taught them; there is beauty in life, just as there is beauty in death. The ravens were noble creatures, smaller kin of the great rocs that lived in the mountains, and had dwelt on Kiavahr longer than man. This was *their* forest, and Shrike knew he would do well to respect that.

He moved, just a fraction, testing himself: one small step, inching around the bough of the tree, never taking his eyes from the bird. He felt the roots of the bolus freeze, and he did the same.

The bird twitched, shaking its wings, and then began pecking at the damp foliage that still clung to the branch, flipping the leaves over with its beak. It was searching for grubs. Not much of a last meal, Shrike mused, but he hoped it would find a juicy one.

He took another step, this time leaving the confines of the tree and edging closer to the bird. Slowly, so as not to attract its attention with sudden movements, he brought his hands together before him, so that they formed a sort of cup, the fingers splayed. He took a third step.

If the bird had noticed him, it showed no sign, continuing to ferret noisily beneath the leaves. A fourth step brought him almost within reach. He could feel the mud squirming between his toes, the dry leaves scratching at his bare ankles, but still he did not make a sound.

The bird jerked its head back suddenly. For a moment he stood, stock still, fearing it was about to take flight, but it had only found a grub and was busy throwing it back down its throat.

Shrike didn't even allow himself a sigh of relief. He took his final step towards the fallen branch, extended his hands, his fingers taught and ready... And a sound from somewhere close by – the snap of a twig underfoot – caused the bird to panic and take flight.

Shrike lurched at it, his fingers brushing its wing, but he was too late, and in a heartbeat it was gone, fluttering off into the treetops.

Furious, he turned on the spot, looking for any sign of the perpetrator, but there was no one there, and the forest was still.

Cursing, Shrike rubbed his shoulders, trying to get the blood circulating quicker, and returned to his spot behind the bolas tree to await his next opportunity.

There was still time.

The Thunderhawk banked sharply, traversing an unexpected patch of turbulence. The vehicle shook so violently that the plasteel substructure in the main hold emitted a loud groan of protest, and a series of impact alarms trilled in the cockpit. The pilot deftly wrestled with the controls, forcing the ship back level, while his co-pilot checked the system monitors, before punching the alarms to silence them. They cut out as suddenly as they had started.

The ship continued its subsonic descent, skimming low over the wreckage of a civilian city and stirring the surface of an abandoned water farm into a frothy churn. Two sister ships, each identical save for white-and-black markings on their wingtips, dipped low alongside it, flying as a unit, as a single wing.

If the enemy knew the Raven Guard had arrived, they'd shown no sign of it; the descending formation of three sleek, black vessels had drawn no fire from the surface of the occupied world.

The sudden jarring caused Shrike to start from his reverie. Distant, half-forgotten memories of Kiavahr dissolved, ephemeral, impossible to cling on to. He let them go. He had a mission to fulfil, and within moments they'd be making planetfall. Now was the time to focus, and to let all thoughts of the past – or future – dissipate. If there was one thing he'd learned during his many decades as a Space Marine of the Raven Guard, it was to live in the here and now. It was the only way to remain alive, and to execute one's mission effectively.

He peered out of the viewing slit, attempting to get a measure of their surroundings. He'd studied hololiths back on the battle-barge, of course – vid-captures of the planet's surface, of the devastation wrought by the marauding xenos – but they'd seemed distant and unreal. Now he was here, on Shenkar, he could see for himself what the greenskins had done.

Shrike was standing in the hold, his power armour mag-locked to the flight-clamps, and he twisted, pulling against his restraints to afford himself a better view. Below the ship, the ruins of countless buildings flitted by, a sea of grey and black, of rubble and burned-out husks, punctuated only by the glowing pyres that still smouldered amongst the remains of the city. Here, great edifices had once been raised to the glory of the Emperor; here, colonnades of immense statues had celebrated the heroes of old; here, the Administratum had overseen the fates of twelve neighbouring worlds. Now, Shenkar was a shell, shattered by an unstoppable tide of green that had swept across the planet's surface, revelling in its utter destruction.

So far, from what Shrike understood, this northern hemisphere had been completely lost, but the legions of the Astra Militarum were hunkered down in the south, bombarding the advancing ork lines with an array of heavy artillery. It was a tenuous position, however, and one that would also soon be lost, without intervention. Shrike had overheard Shadow Captain Saak discussing the matter with one of his sergeants on the battle-barge, and it seemed the Imperium was close to abandoning the planet altogether. The loss would be a grave blow – Shenkar would serve as a staging post for the ork forces to run rampant throughout the entire system, and the Astra Militarum would lose numerous planets that had previously served as recruitment worlds. Additionally, the Shenkar system was a gateway to Imperial space; if the orks managed to gain a foothold here, then further systems would also be at risk.

Shadow Captain Saak had been clear: if the threat was to be contained, it would be contained here, and now.

The role of the Raven Guard was not, as Shrike and his brothers had initially anticipated, to lend reinforcements to the Astra Militarum. Instead, they were to deploy deep behind enemy lines, here amongst the ruins of Shenkar Prime, and attempt to disrupt the ork command. The greenskins were not known for their discipline and organisation, and Saak believed that by cutting off communications from the centre, they would effectively be decapitating the main ork advance. Without command the orks would run riot, and the Astra Militarum would stand a far better chance of breaking their advance and taking back the ruins of the planet. It was an audacious plan, and one forged, Shrike believed, in desperation. Nevertheless, his faith in his captain was unswerving, and he knew without doubt that they would succeed.

Below, the landscape had changed. The once sprawling city was bisected here by a wide gulf, a canyon that had opened up in the substrate, like a gaping wound in the face of the planet. Bleached white chalk – the colour of Shrike's own flesh – was visible, the hidden layers of muscle and sinew that bound the world itself together. The city, it seemed, had been built on a vast plate of impacted chalk, and whatever the orks were now engaged in was rending it apart.

The nose of the Thunderhawk dipped, and Shrike turned away from the viewing slit, regarding his brothers in the hold. There were ten of them back here, as well as the crew up front in the cockpit. All of them wore the gleaming black ceramite of their Chapter, each daubed with kill markings and draped in honour scrolls and ancient Imperial litanies. Bulky jump packs were secured to their backs, and their chainswords and pistols hung ready. Bunches of corvia swung from their belts: the bird-skull totems claimed in the forest as a part of their initiation into the venerable ranks of the Raven Guard, along with those of their fallen battle-brothers, carried as a mark of honour until they might be returned to Kiavahr, and the soil from whence they came.

Directly across from Shrike stood Kadus, his armour mag-locked to the flight-clamps, watching him with a curious expression. His beaked helmet was affixed to his leg brace, and his jaw was set in a mirthless grin. He carried a bright purple scar across the lower half of his face, where he'd once caught the talon of a vicious tyranid creature, before forcing a grenade down its gullet and blowing it apart from the inside. Shrike knew he carried other scars from that encounter, too – not all of them visible.

Beside Kadus was Aarvus, who had also removed his helmet, but was peering out of another viewing slit, his face turned away from Shrike's. Half of Aarvus' head was covered in thick, wiry stubble, while the other was a mess of blistered and bubbled flesh, long healed, but brutally disfiguring. Aarvus had received his injuries during the same campaign as Kadus, fighting tyranids on the icy wastes of Permius IV, and had fallen victim to the hot, acid breath of a genestealer. It had claimed his left eye and right hand before Corus had gunned it down with his bolter. Aarvus rarely spoke of the incident – in fact, he rarely spoke at all, given the state of his lower jaw – but his distaste for xenos was legendary amongst the Third Company, and Shrike suspected he was anticipating planetfall with a grim sense of glee. Corus would have to watch him – he was a fearsome warrior, devoted to his Chapter, but his hatred for the greenskins might prove counterproductive if not properly contained.

Stood beside Aarvus was Gradus, one of the finest warriors Shrike had ever known. A master of infiltration and assassination, he had been responsible for the victory of the squad on too many occasions to count. He'd saved Shrike's life at least twice – that Shrike was aware of – and soon, Shrike was certain, Shadow Captain Saak would reward Gradus with a promotion and his own squad. When the time came, it would be well deserved.

On Shrike's left were Kadryn, Ayros, Arkus, Hirus and Cavaan, five warriors with whom Shrike had served for nearly two decades, and in whose hands he would happily place his fate as surely as those of Captain Saak himself. Now, they each stood silent, patiently anticipating whatever fate awaited them on Shenkar.

Sergeant Corus stood at the rear of the compartment, near to the disembarkation hatch, rocking slightly with the motion of the ship. He must have noticed Shrike looking, for he inclined his head in acknowledgement, before turning away to study the read-out on his auspex.

These were his brothers in arms, his comrades. Together, they had fought across deserts of bone dust and ice, in the bowels of hive cities and the mountainous peaks of airless moons. They'd killed traitors, destroyed xenos nests and liberated entire worlds. They'd fought alongside the Titan legions and Imperial Guard. Now, for the very first time, they were about to undertake a mission against the greenskins; thirty of them, spread across the three gunships, deploying in the midst of thousands.

Shrike knew with a grim certainty that not all of them would leave this planet alive.

The rear disembarkation hatch sighed open to reveal a large, open plaza. To one side, broken pillars grinned unevenly like jagged teeth, while the burned-out husk of an Administratum building still smouldered on the other. The ground here was covered in soot and ash, but had once been smooth, polished marble, and Shrike could still see the outline of the twin-headed Imperial aquila imprinted in it, now partially eclipsed by the footprints of the three Thunderhawks.

Above, the sky was a pale, watery blue, smeared with inky fingerprints of smoke. Black dust swirled around his knees, stirred by the vehicles' cooling engines. He was grateful for the respiratory filter in his helm.

The Thunderhawks had formed a protective laager within the plaza, back-to-back, so that the Space Marines could disembark into the central space, using the gunships as cover. Sentries from Saak's squad had been set up around the perimeter, but as yet had reported no sightings of the enemy. It seemed Saak had chosen his insertion point well; even the contrails of their ships were now lost amongst the columns of smoke rising from the east. The distant rumble of battle would have masked any sound of their approach.

Shrike only hoped their intelligence was correct. The reports had come in from the Militarum Tempestus regarding the probable location of the orks' main command post. He'd have been more comfortable if the reconnaissance had been carried out by the Raven Guard's own Scouts, but he supposed they would have to put their faith in the lesser skills of the humans, and that the orks hadn't moved on in the two days since the report had been filed.

Shadow Captain Saak seemed confident in the humans' abilities, however – or if he wasn't, he was hiding it well. He'd predicated their entire mission on intelligence gleaned from their Tempestor Prime, via a risky surface-to-orbit vox-link. Now, he was gathering the three squads together for their final briefing.

Shrike joined his brothers at the foot of the lead Thunderhawk's disembarkation ramp, upon which Saak now stood, surveying his gathered troops. He was an impressive figure, resplendent in a suit of ancient, ebon armour that dated back to the days of the Great Crusade itself. It was a Chapter relic, worn by innumerable shadow captains of the Third Company over countless centuries, and rumoured to carry their spirits still, imbued within its pitted, burnished surface. Bundles of bleached-white corvia hung from Saak's belt, each and every one of them a reliquary for a dead brother.

'Twelve hours,' began Saak, without ceremony. 'We maintain long-range vox silence. Remember your briefings. Timing is paramount. Your lives, and the lives of your brothers, depend upon it. Take out their power, take out their communication, take out their command.' He stood for a moment, silently looking out across the sea of black helms, and Shrike couldn't shake the feeling that the captain was staring directly at him, weighing him up, judging him.

'Victorus aut mortis,' he said, crossing his arms in their Chapter salute.

'Victorus aut mortis,' murmured Shrike, echoing the captain's salute.

He was part of the squad that would disable the orks' communication network, under the command of Sergeant Corus. The Militarum Tempestus had identified three crude antenna placed at intervals around the city, Shenkar Prime, each feeding the orks' command bunker with reports from the field.

This bunker was, in effect, a warren of caverns carved into a chalk cliff on the outer edge of Shenkar Prime. The city had been built in a vast natural bowl – in theory rendering it more easily defendable – and the cliffs skirted the city in all directions; imposing white sentinels from a distant age.

It was rumoured that the orks' warlord, Gorkrusha, was also operating an experimental weapon from the bunker – a kind of 'seismic agitator,' or earthquake generator, which they'd employed in levelling many of the surrounding structures and disrupting the

Imperial forces. During their earlier briefing they'd been warned of sink-holes and dangerous chasms opening unexpectedly in the ground. He'd heard that the Astra Militarum had lost an entire platoon, heavy artillery and vehicles included, when a major thoroughfare collapsed, dropping them into a river of scolding magma.

Shrike didn't know whether that was fanciful embellishment by the humans, an excuse for their ineptitude, or a truthful representation of what had occurred here on Shenkar. He supposed he would soon find out; Sergeant Corus was gathering his squad now, making ready to deploy.

Shrike's task – along with his brothers – was to blow the transponders within the allotted time, ensuring the bunker was shrouded in a complete blackout when Saak's squad moved in for the final assault. The comms blackout would ensure no warning of the Space Marines' presence here could get to Gorkrusha, giving Saak and his squad a chance to gain entry to the bunker and move freely, taking the entire ork command by surprise. It was a bold plan, but a good one, and Shrike was confident the planet would be as good as liberated by sundown.

He turned at the rumble of distant thunder, looking upwards for any sign of a storm closing in, half expecting to see a squadron of Valkyries flitting overhead, but the skies remained clear and blue.

Frowning, he looked to his brothers, and saw Gradus jabbing his finger towards the ground in warning.

The earth beneath Shrike's boots had begun to tremble, and he could feel a distant thrumming, far below
the surface, like the pounding of a sledge-hammer
against the very core of the world.

The rumbling continued to grow in intensity, making it difficult to maintain his balance. He heard
Corus calling out for them to head to higher ground,
and did as he was ordered, casting around in the
ruins for a more stable position. He found one, clambering up onto a heap of fallen stone.

The rumbling had now reached a crescendo,
and the Space Marines had all scattered, leaving
the plaza empty, save for the three Thunderhawks,
which bucked with the turbulence as if shaken by
the throes of atmospheric re-entry. A rending crack
split the air, originating somewhere deep within the
planet's crust, and one of the Thunderhawks listed
awkwardly, the ground simply falling away beneath
it. Shrike watched in horror as the earth opened its
maw and swallowed the vessel whole.

A moment later the rumbling eased, reduced to
the minor tremor of an aftershock, and Shrike leapt
down from his perch, searching for Kadus and the
others, who had begun to reassemble in the plaza.

They watched Shadow Captain Saak approach the
sink-hole with caution, peering after the missing
vehicle. After a moment, he turned to his troops. 'The
vessel and its crew are lost. Avenge them. Go to it. We
have witnessed here what these xenos are capable of.
We must put an end to them before this day is out.'

'So the rumours are true,' said Kadus, falling in beside Shrike as they filed from the plaza. 'The green-skins have a new weapon.'

'That is no mere weapon,' said Shrike. 'With that machine, they could crack this planet open like an egg – swallow entire battalions. Think what they could do if it were replicated across other worlds.' He glanced at Kadus. 'Whatever it is they're doing here, it has to be destroyed.'

'Then we do as the captain says,' said Kadus. 'We neutralise the transmitters. We shut down their power, and we allow Saak to take out their bunker and their command.'

Shrike nodded. Kadus was right. The mission was more crucial than ever.

They passed through the city like spectres, ghosting from the wreckage of hab-blocks to manufactorums, through deserted streets still echoing with the rever-beration of spent shells, over heaps of turned earth and rubble that had once been other, now indiscern-ible, buildings. Their passage went unremarked, save for the flutter of birds, disturbed by the crunch of their passing boots, and the roar of their jump packs. To even the most vigilant observer, these Space Marines of the Raven Guard would have seemed as nothing but shifting shadows, subtle alterations in the quality of the light as Shenkar's twin suns danced in their odd, elliptical orbit, far off in the void above the planet's surface.

Human corpses littered the alleyways and road-sides, churned by the passing of ork vehicles, or abandoned where they'd fallen to form grisly, decaying heaps. The loss of life here was monumental; this city had once teemed with hundreds of thousands, if not millions of Imperial subjects. Now, aside from small gatherings of refugees hurriedly being evacuated to the south and the Astra Militarum forces engaged against the xenos elsewhere on the continent, the place was devoid of life. The orks had brought their own, peculiar form of destruction to Shenkar, and it was absolute.

Shrike longed to return the compliment. He was spoiling for a fight. Every corpse, every wasted human soul he encountered, was a tally mark, a debt to be repaid by the enemy, and he promised to avenge them all.

There was evidence of the ork weapon here, too – or rather, evidence of the devastation it had wrought. Enormous canyons, some of them stretching for miles, had rent the chalky substrate in two, toppling ancient structures, rupturing fuel pipes and causing aftershocks that would have reduced the city to ruins, were it not for the hail of bombs that had already done the job. Sink-holes had opened up in many of the roads, rendering some of them impassable and forcing Shrike and his brothers to break cover, using their jump packs to boost themselves into the upper reaches of the ruined structures, from which they could clamber over the craters on tentative bridges formed from the iron skeletons of former domiciles. It was almost as if the planet itself were attempting to swallow all signs of human occupation, opening its many mouths to feed.

As they ran, homing in on their target – the first of the communication arrays they'd been tasked with destroying – Shrike noted that an unfamiliar sigil had been daubed across many of the walls and surfaces in brightly coloured paint. The symbol was crude and primitive, resembling nothing so much as a grinning animal face, with two enormous tusks jutting from its lower jaw. This, he presumed, was the glyph of the ork warlord, the one referred to as Gorkrusha. This creature was the driving force behind the orks' rampaging invasion of Shenkar, and the primary target of Shadow Captain Saak's mission when his squad raided the bunker in just a few hours' time.

Out here, in the shattered wreckage of the city, the glyphs were a stamp of ownership, Shrike knew – an attempt by Gorkrusha to lay claim to the planet, marking territory like an alpha-predator. It worked, too; Shrike couldn't shake the feeling that the glyphs had eyes and were silently watching him as he searched out a path in the wreckage, moving ever on towards their next fight.

Static suddenly bubbled in his ear.

'On me! We have live enemy in the road.'

He turned to see Hirus up ahead, raising his bolt pistol. A group of nine orks were clambering out of the tumble-down wreck of a substation by the side of the road – a patrol, perhaps, or a small group of looters. Hirus had drawn them out, of course; the Adeptus Mechanicus who crafted their ebon armour had long ago discovered a means to make it light absorbent, rather than reflective, giving the Raven Guard the aspect of living, ghostly shadows, and ensuring that they were only ever seen when they wished to be.

The orks represented a risk to their mission, however. If they weren't taken out immediately, they might be able to report back before the Space Marines were able to destroy the transmitters, or worse, warn the guards at the transponder stations that they were coming.

Corus knew it, too. His voice crackled over the vox. 'Engage. Make it quick and clean.'

Shrike charged, loosing off a spray of rounds as he barrelled up the road towards the orks, his brothers falling in around him.

The orks, too, wasted no time, their pistols barking as they took pot-shots at the charging Space Marines.

Shrike worked in concert with his brothers, as they had so many times before – fanning out, selecting targets, adopting positions in the road. Within moments, the ebon-armoured warriors had encircled the orks.

Shrike stood his ground as one of the greenskins lumbered towards him. The creature was as tall as Shrike and half as broad again, even taking into account his power armour. Its flesh was a pallid, unnatural green, and it wore sheets of beaten metal, laced together over scraps of clothing. Crude patterns had been daubed across this makeshift armour in bright yellows and reds, and primitive glyphs had been smeared onto the shoulder plates in a strange approximation of the markings on Shrike's own armour. Its hands were the size of a human's head, and in both fists it carried hunks of sharpened metal with bolted-on grips, like axe heads with no attendant haft. Shrike had no doubt that the brute strength of the thing could punch one of those blades through even the toughest war-plate.

The beast's head was enormous, sitting almost uncomfortably on its considerable shoulders, and its face was untamed and savage – not in the way that the wild beasts of Kiavahr were sleek and powerful and primal, but in a raw, brutal, horrifying way. Yellowed tusks jutted from its lower jaw, and its eyes burned with a hate so ferocious that Shrike could almost sense it as a tangible thing. It was monstrous – the enemy of all reason. Shrike knew that he had to kill it, and quickly.

Bolter fire erupted over Shrike's left shoulder, as Arkus engaged one of the other brutes. Shrike followed suit, squeezing the trigger of his own weapon and loosing a shower of bolt shells at the creature before him. They thudded into its armour plating, bursting flesh and spraying gouts of thick, red blood into the air with every impact. The ork, however, seemed undeterred, and with a bellow came bar-relling at him, axe blades held aloft.

Shrike fired off another few rounds from his bolt pistol as the creature closed the gap between them, but this was clearly not a battle that was going to be won with indiscriminate fire. He revved his chainsword and charged, closing the gap between them.

The ork lurched forwards, swinging one of its axe blades down and round in a powerful arc, aiming to split him in two at the midriff. Shrike moved, dodging out of the way and bringing his arm up and forwards, so that his chainsword twisted, glinting between them, opening the ork's face in the process.

It bellowed some obscene curse in its strange, gut-tural language, shaking its head to try to clear the blood that was now streaming into its right eye. The gash had split the creature's face from its cheekbone to its forehead, and Shrike could see bone where the tip of his chainsword had scored its skull. The ork, however, seemed more frustrated than pained by its injuries.

Shrike circled warily, unable to take his eyes off it. The vox suddenly crackled to life in his ear.

'Go for their throats,' said Gradus. 'That's where they seem to be most exposed.'

A quick glance told Shrike that Gradus had man-aged to bring one of the beasts down, and was now assisting Hirus with another.

The glance, however, was all the distraction the

creature needed, and it moved with surprising agility, surging forwards and catching Shrike unprepared with a sudden upward blow from its axe. The force of the strike lifted Shrike from his feet, sending him careening backwards into the air, so that he collided with a broken pillar that was lying in the road. Warning sigils flashed up inside his helm. He blinked them away, suppressing the pain. Luckily, the axe hadn't opened his armour. He might not be so fortunate the next time, however – the ork was advancing again, both blades raised above its head, ready to cleave him apart.

Shrike leapt sideways as the ork closed in, its axes smashing down into the stone pillar with an echoing crunch. The pillar cracked, splintering apart in a shower of dust.

Shrike rounded on it, just in time to see Cavaan launch himself at the ork from behind, burying his combat knife between the creature's shoulder-blades. It roared and spun, whirling its axes and catching Cavaan in the shoulder as he leapt back. His pauldron burst in a shower of adamantium, and dark, arterial blood arced into the air, spattering the ork's face and staining the parched earth.

Cavaan staggered back, fumbling for his bolt pistol, while the ork flexed its shoulders, trying to shake the combat knife loose. Shrike could see the weapon now, jutting out between two sheets of its thick armour plating. The blade had clearly struck home; the creature was more agitated even than when he'd turned its face to ribbons with his chainsword.

Cavaan was still backing away, his bolt pistol gripped in his good arm, but the ork had now turned its attentions to him and was advancing menacingly.

Shrike activated his jump pack with a sudden roar. He felt the surge of power at his back, pushing him down, and fought the urge to angle his body upwards. He shot forwards like a loosed bolt-round. His dipped shoulder collided with the ork's back, square between the shoulder-blades, throwing the creature forcefully to the ground, and sending Shrike off into a wild spiral, twisting through the air, until he cut the power and came tumbling back down in a heap, close to where Cavaan was standing. The injured Space Marine regarded him with what Shrike could only assume was bemusement.

'An unusual tactic, brother,' said Cavaan, holding out his good hand and hauling Shrike to his feet.

The shock of the impact had caused more warning sigils to flare inside Shrike's helm, but he blinked them away. He was still clutching his chainsword, and he held it out before him as he approached the prone ork. As he drew nearer, he could see that the impact had forced Cavaan's blade clean through the creature's chest and out the other side, splintering its ribs. It wasn't breathing. He lowered his chainsword. 'I'll allow you the pleasure of recovering your own blade,' he said, without hiding his distaste.

'My thanks,' said Cavaan.

Shrike surveyed the scene. The road was littered with corpses. Mercifully, they all appeared to be xenos. The fight had been more brutal than any one of them could have anticipated.

His brothers were regrouping beneath the cover of a nearby hab-block, the upper storeys of which had been destroyed during some previous, hellish battle. He went to join them, Cavaan at his side.

Corus was consulting his auspex, and he looked up as Shrike approached. 'Target acquired,' he said. 'Over that ridge to the west, about half a mile. Kadus, Shrike, Cavaan, Aarvus, Gradus – circle around to the far side and take up positions. Ayros, Kadryn, Hirus, Arkus, with me. We close in on their position like a tightening noose. When I give the order, move in and set the place alight.' He paused for a beat. 'Understood?'

'Understood,' echoed Shrike, along with his brothers.

He turned to see Kadus already making a bee-line for the ridge, beckoning for him and the others to follow.

Shrike peered over the lip of a fallen tree, study-ing their target and its attendant xenos guards. His bolt pistol was trained on the nearest ork, and he was ready to put a round into its throat at the slight-est provocation. There were twelve of the brutish creatures milling about in the vicinity of the com-munications array, wearing makeshift armour and carrying snub-nosed pistols and chainblades. They appeared to be distracting themselves by taunting a smaller, skittish, green-skinned creature, whose sole purpose seemed to be to provide entertainment for the guards. Its big ears flapped unhappily as it received another booted foot in the ribs and went sprawling in the dirt, eliciting another round of hideous, rasping laughter.

The communications array was a bristling spire of antenna masts and aerials, at the centre of a nest of powercells and cables. It had once been of human construction, feeding official transmissions out across the city, but now it had been co-opted by the xenos. Their primitive technology had been spliced in and bolted on, hijacking the main rig and redirecting the traffic, on a frequency the Astra Militarum had found almost impossible to intercept. Even if they had managed it, Shrike mused, he couldn't imagine they'd have understood much of what they'd heard.

To his left, Cavaan lay hunkered down amongst the foliage of the downed tree, the nose of his bolt pistol just visible to Shrike's trained eyes. To his right, Gradus was similarly positioned, pressed flat amongst the exposed roots, ready to swoop in as soon as Corus gave the order.

Shrike scanned the far side of the aerial cluster for any sign of the others. Nothing. Seven of the orks were still busying themselves with the runt, while the others appeared to be engaged in a game involving bone dice and fists. Now would be the perfect time to act.

He decided to risk a short burst on the vox.

'Sergeant?' he whispered, his voice barely audible inside his helm.

'Hold your position, Shrike,' came the terse response.

Shrike squeezed the grip of his bolt pistol a little tighter, but did as Corus had ordered. The orks were growing tired of their sport, however, and he could see the moment was going to pass. He wondered what Corus was waiting for; no doubt something that Shrike himself couldn't see. Perhaps he was just being impatient.

The vox crackled to life again a moment later. 'Go.'

Shrike sprang up into a crouch with a subtlety and grace that seemed incongruent with his armoured bulk. Around him, his brothers did the same, forming a ring around the small encampment.

Their jump packs roared as they powered into the air, swooping down on the unsuspecting orks, who, stirred by the sudden noise, abandoned their games and leapt to their feet, reaching for their weapons.

The runt, clutched over the shoulder of one of the orks who had his back to Shrike, gave a sudden squeal of alarm, waving its arms in an ungainly, excited fashion. Shrike caved in its pathetic skull with a single round.

Another shot punctured the back of the ork's neck, blowing a hole in its throat, and the chainsword stirred to life in Shrike's fist as he dropped to the ground, ripping through the ork's chest to finish it off before it had even drawn its weapon.

Shrike twisted at a guttural roar from behind him

to see another ork launch itself at Ayros, its chainblade skewering the Space Marine between the
shoulder-blades, rending his jump pack and bursting from his chest in a shower of blood and cartilage.
Ayros screamed, a visceral, rending cry that rever-
berated across the vox, as the chainblade carved his
innards to pulp.

The ork gave a grunting snort that Shrike took to
be a laugh, as it lifted the impaled Ayros on its blade,
causing him to gurgle and vomit blood that seeped
out beneath his helm.

As the dying Ayros slumped back onto the sword,
falling into the gleeful ork, he thumbed the detonator
on a krak grenade in his fist. There was a moment's
pause, and then the grenade exploded.

Shrike recoiled from the blast, staggering back as
the force of it hit him. When he looked again a second later, all that was left was the steaming lower
half of the ork, lying in a perfectly smooth crater,
and a handful of black fragments that had once been
armour.

Sound and light erupted all around him in stuttering bursts as the rest of the Raven Guard stirred
to life, dropping from the sky, bolt pistols barking,
chainswords raging.

Shrike circled the transmitter, spraying a cluster of
three orks with a hail of fire, shredding the face of one
in the process. Its limp, lifeless body slumped to the
floor, its skull shattered by the impact of the shells.

Another ork fell, too, its face a mess of bubbling

wounds as an explosive round blew out its left eye socket, while another opened a fist-sized hole in its throat. It dropped to its knees, emitting a wet gurgle, before collapsing face down in the dirt.

Shrike realised Corus was bellowing commands over the vox. 'Shrike. Blow the transmitter.'

'Sergeant,' he acknowledged, levelly.

He edged around the antenna cluster, keeping his fire concentrated on another of the orks, which was taking pot shots at Gradus and Hirus as they tried to circle around it, trapping it between them. A lucky round found its mark, blowing the creature's hand clean away from the stump of its wrist and sending its pistol spinning into the dust in a spray of blood and fingers. It howled in pain, glancing in disbelief at the ruin of its appendage, just as Gradus launched himself at it, his chainsword severing its throat so deep that he almost lifted its head from its shoulders. They both went down heavily in a tangle of thrashing limbs.

Shrike moved. Three steps took him to the central column of the array. Warning sigils flared inside his helm as a stray round from a pistol scored the back of his vambrace, but he ignored it.

All around him the chatter of bolter fire, the roar of the xenos, the battle-cries of his brothers, the sound of chainblades chewing into ceramite – they merged into a cacophony, a discordant symphony of war. It made his pulse quicken and his blood sing. He longed to turn, to let loose on the filthy xenos who had taken Ayros, to join his brothers in the heat of battle. The more of the orks he could take down, the better. Yet he knew the mission was paramount. Shadow Captain Saak was depending on them.

Carefully, Shrike clambered over the lower stanchions of the rig, searching for a suitable location. He found it near the base of the secondary column, amidst a bundle of winking diodes: a control matrix or transmission exchange.

'Get clear!' he bellowed, as he primed a krak grenade and dropped it into the nest of wires. He stepped back, and turned directly into the path of a buzzing chainblade.

The ork stood over him, spittle dripping from its massive jaws. One of its teeth was freshly broken, and blood streamed from a gash in its upper arm. The chest-plate of its armour was splashed with crimson gore that Shrike was sure was not its own. Another of his brothers had fallen to this beast.

Shrike twisted, but the ork moved with surprising speed, and the chainblade bit deep into his left pauldron. Alarms buzzed, and Shrike pulled back, trying to put some space between himself and the blade. The ragged teeth of the chainsword had chewed deep into his armour, though, and as much as he attempted to lurch back, he couldn't free himself of its bite. The krak grenade was going to detonate at any moment.

The ork laughed, revving the blade slowly, taunting him as it slowly ripped through the final layer of ceramite and scored a deep cut into Shrike's upper arm. He clenched his jaw, fighting against the surging pain, and kicked out at the ork, catching it square in the chest with his boot. The blow struck with such force that it dented the metal plate and staggered the creature.

This retaliation did little to dissuade it, but that had not been Shrike's intention; he was merely buying himself a second to consider his options. His combat knife was still in its sheath, but getting close enough to use it without losing his arm would be problematic. He could detonate another grenade, just as Ayros had, but he couldn't risk the obvious sacrifice, not with two further arrays still to be destroyed, and a ticking chrono working against them.

He'd have to lose the arm, then. Go for the knife, allow the arm to be severed, and take the ork's jugular as it struggled to free its trapped blade. About to act, Shrike paused in surprise, as another ebon-handled combat knife whistled past his head, burying itself in the creature's right eye.

The ork released its grip on the chainsword, both hands going up to its face, but the knife had been thrown with tremendous force, and had burst the eye, the tip of its blade coming to rest deep inside the creature's brain. It scrabbled for a moment, trying to pull the blade free, before one of its legs gave way, and it slumped to the ground in a heap.

Shrike powered his jump pack and shot into the air

as the rig blew in his wake, the krak grenade toppling the main antenna array with an explosive crump.

Shrike set himself down, stumbling onto one knee on the uneven ground. He twisted to see Corus standing close by, pulling his combat knife free of the smouldering ork corpse, implacable behind the mask of his beaked helm.

'My thanks to you, sergeant,' he said. He indicated the chainblade still buried in his pauldron. 'If you'd do me the honour?'

Corus walked over, grabbing the handle of the weapon. 'Prepare yourself,' he said, and then fingered the trigger. The blade roared to life again, and pain flared in Shrike's shoulder. He was glad he was wearing his helm, lest he display his discomfort to his sergeant.

Corus yanked on the blade, pulling it free from the deep scar in Shrike's armour. He tossed it, still churning, into the nest of cables at his feet, causing sparks to pop and flare from where several of the power leads were severed. Smoke curled from the ruins of the array.

Shrike could feel blood flowing freely down the arm of his power armour, now, pooling at the wrist. Almost immediately, however, his enhanced circulatory system flooded the wound with analgesics and clotting fluids, stemming the blood loss and numbing the pain. He flexed it experimentally. It still worked. It would heal soon enough.

Around them, the last of the orks were engaged

with three Space Marines apiece, and Shrike could see the tide had already turned in the Raven Guard's favour. Another of his brothers – Kadryn – lay dead close by, his body neatly carved from shoulder to hip. Shrike allowed himself a momentary pang of regret.

'Time to move out,' said Corus. 'Finish them.'

Shrike took up his chainsword, ready to join his brothers.

'Not you,' said Corus, holding out a staying hand. 'You retrieve Kadryn's corvia. His gene-seed will burn with this rig, but it is our duty to honour him still. Today, that burden is yours, Shrike.'

'I accept it with honour, sergeant,' said Shrike.

Chainsword in hand, he crossed to where Kadryn's remains lay in a growing pool of his internal fluids. They were mingling with the dust, already beginning to congeal. Shrike surveyed the corpse dispassionately. Kadryn's torso had almost been severed in two by a chainsword similar to the one that had carved up his own shoulder, and the ragged-edged wound glistened with fresh, weeping gore. Shrike suppressed his rage. Kadryn had done his duty, as had Ayros, and thousands of others before them. Just as Shrike himself would do without a moment's hesitation.

'I will honour you, brother, in the forests of Kiavahr. I shall restore your corvia to the ground from whence they came. Your sacrifice was not in vain.' He reached down and, using his combat knife, cut the tiny bundle of raven skulls free from Kadryn's belt. He held them up to the light, counting seven of them, before standing and tying them to his own belt, adding them to the growing number that hung there. The company had lost many in recent months, and he hoped that before long they would return to Kiavahr to pay tribute, and to swell their ranks with more worthy initiates.

He turned at the sound of another strangled death cry, to see the last of the orks crumple, two chainswords jutting from its thick neck.

'Move out,' said Corus, quietly.

Shrike heard no murmur of argument from the others.

He didn't look back.

The second array was housed in what could only be described as a fortified bunker: a squat, plascrete building with a single door. The only other apertures were thin viewing slits cut at regular intervals around the structure. The powercells, they had discerned, were all inside the bunker, with only a handful of aerials jutting through a small opening in the roof. The place was swarming with orks. There were more than twenty of the creatures, armed with a motley assortment of weapons, including what appeared to be primitive rocket launchers and guns that were the analogues of Imperial flamers.

Following a brief reconnaissance, the Raven Guard had holed up in the ruins of an Administratum building a short distance from the bunker. From here, they were better able to observe the xenos without drawing unwanted attention, while they formulated their plan.

Hirus and Gradus had taken up defensive positions on the upper gantry, searching the surrounding ruins for any sign of further xenos. Shrike was sure that none of the greenskins they'd engaged thus far had shown enough intelligence to vox for reinforcements – and, indeed, the creatures seemed arrogant enough to believe that a small contingent of Space Marines offered little threat – but there was always the risk that the orks had now noticed that one of their rigs had gone down, and were sending out reinforcements to protect the others. This one certainly seemed to be well attended.

'We could take out the aerials with long-range fire,' ventured Kadus. 'Short, concentrated bursts from multiple directions. The orks wouldn't know who was attacking them. We'd have a chance to bring the aerials down and then melt away before they found us.'

Corus nodded. 'I can see the sense in such an approach, but the aerials themselves are not enough. It would be a small matter for the orks to erect a secondary mast and reinstate the array. We have to take out the transmitter itself.'

'Then that means getting inside,' said Kadus.

'Not necessarily,' said Shrike. 'We lay down suppressing fire. Keep the enemy pinned inside the bunker, while two of us get close. If we can get enough krak grenades through those apertures, we can blow the whole structure from within, taking out the orks as well as the transmitter.'

'It's risky,' said Kadus. 'We're not armed for that type of suppressing fire.'

'Yes,' said Corus. 'But we've delayed too long already. Time is not on our side. Shrike – can you do this?'

Shrike nodded. 'Yes, sergeant.' He glanced at Kadus.

'Then I shall join you, brother,' he said.

'Aye,' said Corus. He beckoned to Cavaan, who'd been maintaining watch on the bunker from behind a broken doorway. 'Gather the others. We're moving out.'

'When I give the order, concentrate all of your fire on that doorway,' voxed Corus. 'If even one of those damned xenos gets out, we're in trouble. Stop at nothing to keep them pinned while Shrike and Kadus do their work.'

Shrike listened to the chorus of acknowledgements as he crept through the brittle, fire-damaged undergrowth that served as the only cover between his current position and the bunker itself. The bastion was situated at the centre of a large, open plaza – previously a commemorative square or gathering place – providing the orks with an easily defendable position. Shrike guessed it must have once been an outpost for the Adeptus Arbites policing the capital city here on Shenkar.

He folded himself into the shadows by the blackened

stump of a tree, and waited. A quick glance across the plaza told him that Kadus had also found himself an appropriate position; Shrike couldn't discern him amongst the blasted landscape.

There were presently two orks standing in the mouth of the open doorway, weapons slung casually low. They didn't appear to be expecting an ambush. If anything, Shrike decided, they looked bored. That could be dangerous – if they were spoiling for a fight, then keeping them pinned to the bunker might prove difficult. Nevertheless, Shrike had a keen sense of time slipping away from them. They'd have to move soon if they were to blow the third transmitter in time.

Corus' voice barked in his ear. 'Now!'

From the other side of the plaza, the Raven Guard opened fire. A hail-storm of rounds showered the bunker, concentrated around the open door. One of the orks fell back, returning fire indiscriminately into the ruins, while the other buckled, explosive rounds tearing chunks from its face and chest until it crumpled and fell.

The noise was incredible as the bolt shells hammered against the plascrete, pounding the frame with such explosive ferocity that chunks of it dislodged and crumbled to the ground. Shrike heard a series of sharp, orkish bellows from inside the bunker, and seconds later the chatter and flare of returning fire burst to life in the doorway. This was all the distraction he was going to get.

Shrike leapt to his feet, clutching a krak grenade in each hand. Keeping his head down, he ran towards the bunker, his feet kicking up clouds of dust in his wake. Rounds hissed in the air all around him, distracting, causing him to duck and weave, but still he stayed on course, charging head on for the enemy, seeing only the target – the open doorway.

He was only yards away from the bunker when he realised they'd miscalculated. Another ork had circled the bunker and was now hunkered down just a short distance away, training what appeared to be a missile launcher on him. He saw a brief flare of ignition in the periphery of his vision, followed by a high-pitched whine, and knew that he only had seconds to act.

He launched into the air on a plume of flame as the projectile smashed home, striking the bunker wall and detonating with an enormous, incendiary blast. Acting purely on instinct, Shrike thumbed the detonators on the krak grenades and hurled them in the direction of the ork, which watched them land by its feet with a curious expression, before they exploded and smeared the greenskin across the ground in at least five different directions.

Shrike heard the crump of another detonation, this time inside the bunker. Kadus was evidently having more success. He dropped to the ground, grabbing two further grenades from his belt, and leapt at the bunker, slamming them both through the nearest aperture.

This time the ground itself shook as they went off, and black smoke curled from the small hole in the roof, along with the oily stench of charred meat.

The distant bark of bolter fire died off.

'Finish it off, Kadus,' said Shrike. His injured shoulder was screaming in protest. He took a step back from the bunker. The bolter fire flared again. Shrike turned to see a shadow in the mouth of the doorway, slowly emerging into the light.

The ork was a towering wall of green flesh encased in red-and-black armour, bigger than any other he'd seen. Its left arm was missing, the wound cauterised from the heat of the explosion that had removed it. The skin of its face was charred and smouldering, and steam rose from its armour plating, where it had fused with the creature's chest. It staggered out into the plaza, bolt-rounds thudding relentlessly into its hide. It shook its head groggily, and then turned and looked right at him, gimlet eyes peering out from beneath the burned ridge of its forehead.

Shrike reached for his bolt pistol as the ork flexed its neck, raising its remaining fist. For a moment the two of them – Space Marine and ork – regarded one another, sizing each other up as if they were the only two combatants on the entire planet, and then the ork charged, and Shrike let rip with his pistol, hammering the thing in the face as it ran.

It closed the gap in seconds, swinging its gargantuan fist in a wide arc and landing a blow that lifted Shrike from his feet, sending him skittering across the plaza on his back. Behind him, he heard another explosion as Kadus tossed the final charges into the burning wreckage of the bunker. Breathless, Shrike scrabbled to his feet, feeling for his chainsword.

The ork was half dead – that much was clear from the shambolic way it moved, from the seared, peeling flesh of its face and the blood flowing freely from the deep gash in its abdomen; yet it seemed intent on finishing him off before it succumbed to its mortal wounds. It lumbered towards him, ignoring the spray of bolter fire chewing up its back, stooping to sweep up a hunk of broken plascrete into its massive fist. It intended to cave his skull in with it, and judging by the look of its upper arm, Shrike knew that a single blow to the head would leave him reeling and delirious, despite his helm.

He edged back, keeping pace with the beast, observing its every move in order to anticipate its next attack. They were circling the bunker now, putting the creature out of line of sight of his brothers. Their covering fire had once again ceased, and the vox-channel hissed silently in his ear. Shrike knew they weren't about to join the fray; the mission was too critical, and time was too precious. If he were Corus, he'd have already started moving out, leaving the injured Shrike to keep the remaining ork engaged, and thus allowing the others to escape unhindered. That was protocol – move on to the next target as swiftly and efficiently as possible. Shrike would be sacrificed for the benefit of the mission.

None of this troubled him. He would gladly die to protect his brothers, and to ensure the completion of their mission. He was damned if he was going down without a fight, however.

The ork came at him, swinging the rock up and around in an effort to knock him off balance once again. Shrike had anticipated the move, though, and leapt out of the way, neatly sidestepping the movement. While the ork attempted to recover its own balance, he darted forwards and slashed its remaining arm with his chainsword, rending a deep, ragged wound that caused the creature to drop the rock and stagger back, howling in rage.

He could see it was beginning to slow as its injuries began to get the better of it. If he could keep it going just a little longer, he might be able to get close enough to do some real harm.

Beneath him, the ground seemed to suddenly shift, and he staggered, fighting to regain his balance. At first he thought the orks were firing their seismic weapon again, but a quick glance told him it was just the bunker, the supports finally giving out under the stress of the explosions. One of the walls had crumbled, and the roof was beginning to collapse. He sidestepped to avoid a sliding hunk of plascrete, just as the ork's fist connected with his head.

Shrike staggered back, his mind reeling. He tried to focus, but blackness limned the edge of his vision. He blinked, concentrating on the flashing sigils inside his helm, trying to read their warnings as another blow hit home, and he dropped to one knee, delirium threatening to close in on him. He closed his eyes, and the world spun.

Think of the forest. The forest is everything.

Shrike drew a ragged, stuttering breath. For a moment, he was back on Kiavahr, back amongst the soaring boughs and leafy expanse of the forest. He could almost smell the damp earth in his nostrils, feel the cool breeze on his body, the excitement of the hunt.

Then he opened his eyes again, and reality rushed in.

The ork was about to deliver its final blow. Shrike knew he would not survive another. Still dazed, he glanced down at his hands. His chainsword had gone, lost somewhere amongst the rubble of the bunker. Broken lintels and collapsed walls lay all around him, accompanied by the electrical stench of burning machinery. The smouldering humps of dead orks lay amongst the wreckage. And beside him, just a yard away, was the jagged, broken spire of the antenna cluster from the roof.

Shrike lurched, grabbing for the makeshift lance. His gauntleted fingers closed around it, and he snatched it up from the dust. He twisted, planting one end of it in the ground before him and holding the other forwards, like a pike, bracing himself for impact.

Too late, the ork saw what was coming, but was unable to slow the considerable momentum of its attack. It came at him, swinging its fist, only to find itself skewered on the end of the antenna, puncturing its chest.

Shrike held his ground, his hands trembling with the force, as the ork's momentum carried it forwards, sliding further onto the metal lance. Shrike could smell its hot, rancid breath as it leaned in, its tusks only inches from the beak of his helm. Thick blood was oozing down the shaft of the antenna, but Shrike's hands were pinned beneath the bulk of the creature. He couldn't move.

The ork made a sound that might have been a rasping laugh, and then pulled its head back and slammed it forwards into Shrike's helm, jarring him suddenly backwards. He felt the world closing in.

Everything went black.

Shrike woke with a start. He gasped for breath, filling his lungs.

He was lying on his back. It was still daylight. Above, he could see birds, wheeling against a pale blue sky punctuated with distant vapour trails and drifting columns of smoke.

For a moment, he was unsure where he was. He tried moving, but pain blossomed in his shoulder. He waited a moment for the sensation to subside and then sat up. Beside him, the corpse of an enormous ork lay in the still-burning ruins of a bunker, the shaft of a metal antenna erupting from its back. Blood and vomit lay in puddles all around it. The creature had suffered a bad death. He glanced at his hands; they were covered in blood.

Shrike took another deep breath, flexing his neck and shoulders. He shook his head, trying to clear the fog.

Shenkar. The communications arrays. The mission.

How long had he been unconscious?

Shrike got to his feet. He cancelled the alarms shrilling inside his helm. His shoulder was repairing itself, but the arm would be weak for some hours. He'd suffered an array of minor injuries, but nothing serious, and his clarity seemed to be returning.

'Sergeant?' He spoke into the vox. 'Kadus?'

The only response was the crackle of uninterrupted static. The others had moved on, continuing with the mission. He considered extending the range of the vox, attempting to make contact with his squad, but he knew that long-range vox-casts were against orders and risked drawing the attention of the orks. He'd have to rendezvous with them at the location of the third transmitter.

Shrike activated a sigil in his retinal display and pulled up a topographical map of the area – pre-invasion – and the anticipated site of the final target.

With a final look around to ensure he wasn't being observed, he crossed the plaza at a run, and melted into the shadows of the nearby ruins.

Shrike followed the road for some time as it looped around the shells of hab-blocks and manufactorums, keeping to the shadows, but soaring for extended periods using his jump pack, intent on catching up with his brothers. So far, he'd seen no evidence of their passing, but that was only to be expected.

Presently, the road opened out into another large forum – previously the site of a commercial district, judging by the iconography of its ruined buildings – but now the desolate wasteland of a former warzone. Here, the Astra Militarum had confronted the orks, and lost. Nests of razor wire and gun emplacements, churned bunkers and heaped sandbags marked their passing.

The stillness of the place was eerie; not even the birds seemed to stir here. It was as if an echo of the violence that had taken place here remained, evidenced by the battered shell of a Baneblade, along with two crashed Valkyries, and the grinning, mechanised horror of an orkish war machine, now listing against the corner of a wrecked tower. It was an engine of pure destruction, forged from the wicked imagination of the xenos' engineers, and shaped to resemble what Shrike took to be an effigy of their heathen god. It was a patchwork of salvaged components, most of them indistinguishable from junk, aside from the chassis of an old Rhino, bolted into its skirts, and an autocannon stripped from an Imperial Knight, now mounted in a makeshift housing.

Nevertheless, the machine had been brought down, or at least halted, by the Imperial forces; numerous holes in its armoured casing paid testament to their work. The orks must have swept through here in their multitudes, however, for the half-rotten corpses of the Astra Militarum soldiers lay all around him, in plain sight, dragged from their tanks and vehicles, butchered where they lay. Dead orks rotted in their midst, their armour looted by their brethren. Civilians, too, had died here, for the evacuation had come too slowly, and the orks had arrived first, massacring everything that moved. Now, every available surface had been daubed with the same glyph he had seen earlier – the grinning, animalistic face – and he longed to put an end to the creature whose visage it represented.

Shrike felt as if he could read the ebb and flow of the battle that had played out here, and it sickened him. He was certain his brothers would have felt the same as they'd passed this way, lending fervour to their resolve. Shenkar *would* be liberated. The ork menace would be quashed.

Shrike felt a deep, bass rumble beneath his boots and glanced down the road in the direction from which he'd come. The sound reminded him of the approach of incoming tanks, and for a moment he wondered whether the Astra Militarum were returning, or else another of the strange ork war machines was making its way back to the ork base camp. There was nothing coming, however, and as the rumbling intensified, Shrike recognised it for what it was: the orks were using their seismic weapon again.

He turned and jumped – deciding haste was

preferable to cover, particularly as any shelter was liable to come down on top of him as the impact of the weapon was magnified. The ground was shaking now, the entire substrate trembling as the weapon agitated the tectonic structure of the continent.

Shrike stumbled, almost going down, as a crack appeared in the road surface, grinning open like a toothless smile. Somewhere close by, deeper into the maze of the city, another building collapsed, its foundations shaken so violently that its ancient walls crumbled. The noise of rending stone was horrendous, blotting out all else, leaving Shrike feeling under siege and senseless. To him, the ork weapon was anathema. The Raven Guard operated through subtlety and stealth, striking from the shadows to eliminate their targets; this xenos weapon rendered that near impossible. It was vulgar, brash, and utterly deadly. It would level the entire planet, destroying everything the Imperium had built here over centuries of occupation. And to what end? What did the orks even hope to achieve here? They revelled in destruction for its own sake, and in their ignorance, saw power in such acts. It was the logic of primitives, and it could not be reasoned with or dissuaded. Only an equal or greater show of force could resolve this. The battle had to be taken to the orks.

Shrike ran on. Sink-holes were opening up in the road all around him as the ork weapon smashed a new channel through the broken streets. Plumes

of chalk dust burst into the air like volcanic erup-
tions, as the very ground fought itself, cracking and
rending, threatening to swallow him at any moment.
Buildings were subsiding all around him now, sliding into the earth. One of the abandoned tanks,
still armed, exploded as it was forced into a newly
opened crevasse, its crushed plasma shells erupting
in a searing spray.

Up ahead, a toppling structure threatened to block
the road, and Shrike boosted higher, soaring over a
steel girder as plascrete blocks tumbled down behind
him, spilling across the broken rockcrete.

He landed on the other side to carnage of apoca-
lyptic proportions.

From here he could see for miles in all directions.
This whole sector of the city had been levelled by
the seismic quakes, with only a handful of partial
structures still standing, intermittent spokes against
a sky-line of burning rubble.

Enormous channels criss-crossed the landscape,
acres wide and deep enough that magma was swill-
ing up from the core of the planet to form molten
rivers inside them. All thoughts of liberation fled
from Shrike's mind, then. Shenkar was ruined, rendered utterly uninhabitable. All he could see was the
grinning, painted face of the creature who had done
this to this world, who had daubed his image across
a thousand ruins, taunting the Imperial forces with
his omnipotence. Shrike vowed that if Shadow Captain Saak was unable to end its miserable life here

on Shenkar, then *he* would do it, somehow. The galaxy could not stand for the abhorrent thing to live.

'...ther...garri...serg...'

Shrike started as his vox suddenly crackled to life in his ear. He hadn't been able to make out the words, but he'd evidently come within range of the others.

'Sergeant?' he said urgently. 'Sergeant Corus?'

'Shrik...' came the response. 'Is tha...' It trailed off into a fuzz of unintelligible static.

He was within a mile of the site of the third transmitter. Clearly the others were closing in on the target, too.

Clutching his bolt pistol, he boosted into the sky again, soaring above the wreckage. For now, there was only one thing on his mind: find the others, and complete the mission.

He located Kadus first, surveying an enormous rent in the ground, less than half a mile from the ruins of the commercial district. The rest of the squad were stretched out along the line of the crevasse, each of them searching for a suitable place to make a crossing.

'So, there *are* such things as ghosts,' said Kadus, when he saw Shrike approaching. He clasped him on the shoulder. 'It's good to see you, brother. We thought you lost.'

'For a while, Kadus, I thought I was lost too.'

'I wished to go back for you, but Corus forbade it.'

'Then he showed great wisdom,' said Shrike. 'The

greenskins are a scourge that must be eradicated. No single life is worth saving for that. And no corvia, for that matter.'

Kadus nodded his assent. 'Still, I'm impressed you took down that beast, even if it did only have one arm.'

Shrike laughed. 'I fear these greenskins are hardy creatures,' he said, 'and that Saak's assassination of their command will be hard won.'

'Not least if we cannot find a means to bypass that crevasse,' said Kadus. 'You felt the effects of the enemy weapon, I presume?'

'I felt the earth itself tremble in fear,' said Shrike. 'This weapon is a planet killer. If they are not stopped soon, this rock and everything upon it will be utterly torn asunder.'

He peered over the lip of the crevasse. The ground had ceased its trembling now, aside from the distant rumble of aftershocks, and the true scale of the devastation wrought by the ork weapon was only now becoming evident. The chasm was a hundred yards wide, its jagged white cliffs descending into nothingness. Gouts of bubbling magma spurted from rents in the cliff-face, searing the chalk and setting all else in its path ablaze. The canyon stretched away into the distance in both directions, running through the very heart of the once-great city.

Shrike consulted his retinal display. The target was on the other side, almost directly ahead. 'Then we go around,' he said.

Kadus shook his head. He pointed to the east. 'The canyon stretches for seven miles in that direction before it becomes passable. There's no time.' He turned. 'And that way lies an enemy garrison. It's just as impassable as the canyon, if we want to live.'

'Then we go over,' said Shrike.

'You know as well as I do that our jump packs can't carry us that far.'

'What does Corus say?'

'Corus says it's good to see you still standing, Shrike.' Shrike turned to see the sergeant standing behind him, his head cocked slightly to one side.

'Sergeant,' said Shrike, in acknowledgement.

'Brother Kadus is correct in his assertion,' said Corus.

'Then what of Shadow Captain Saak and the others – are we simply to send them to their deaths?'

'The captain will see that we have failed. He will halt his advance and regroup at the appointed rendezvous. There was only ever a slim chance we could succeed in this mission.' Corus stood defiant.

'Failure has never been an option,' said Shrike. 'It is not an option now. Better that we all die than admit defeat.'

'You have your orders,' said Corus.

'We cannot simply give up,' said Shrike.

Kadus put a hand on Shrike's pauldron. 'The sergeant has spoken, Kayvaan. He's heard what you have to say.'

'This is not our way. This has *never* been our way.' Shrike knew that he had overstepped, that he was guilty of grave insubordination, but he'd remained silent for too long. Corus was a worthy warrior, and had claimed great victories for the Chapter, but he had never been a strong leader. Ever since childhood, since their early days on Kiavahr, before the Raven Guard had come for them, Corus had always been reluctant to take risks.

'You've seen what they've done to this world, Shrike,' said Corus. 'There is nothing left to fight over. The planet is lost. The Astra Militarum will be ordered to pull out, and the Chapter Master will sanction a full Exterminatus.' Corus reached up and unclipped his helm. It sighed as the pressure equalised with the external environment. He pulled it off, fixing Shrike with a hard stare. His ebon eyes shone like mirrors, reflecting Shrike's battered, bedraggled form back at him. His jaw was set firm. 'This is our way. The planet will be cleansed.'

'With respect, sergeant, the greater imperative is whether Gorkrusha is allowed to escape and deploy his seismic weapon on another Imperial world. Exterminatus will take too long. Whatever he is doing here, he must be close to his end goal. You are right – we're too late to save Shenkar, but what of the other worlds that might follow? Do you want a billion more deaths on your conscience? Gorkrusha has to be stopped, here, on Shenkar. We have to clear the way for Shadow Captain Saak.'

'*Shrike,*' said Kadus, in warning. 'You go too far. Stand down.'

'No, Kadus. What if we had simply given up on each other, all those years ago on Kiavahr? What then? Aren't we stronger because we understand the need to work together? Shadow Captain Saak is relying on us. We do our duty in the name of the Emperor. We *must* go on. We do not have a choice.'

Corus was looking contemplative. He glanced at Kadus. 'Perhaps he has a point. From Shenkar, this Gorkrusha could deploy his weapon to the entire system. The devastation would be unconscionable.'

'Thank you, sergeant,' said Shrike. 'I believe we can find a means to cross. Down there,' he pointed to a ridge on the far side of the canyon, 'is a ledge wide enough to receive us all. Our jump packs can get us across that far. Then it's a simple matter of scaling the chalk to reach the other side.'

Corus shook his head. 'Kadus has already assessed that jump. The likelihood is that less than half of us would survive, Shrike. Some of us, you included, are carrying grievous wounds. Those who did make it would stand little chance against any xenos we encountered on the other side. If we do this, we go around.'

'We can make it. If we go around, we'll be too late. The captain will have already deployed by the time we reach the transmitter. It's a seven-mile detour before we can even make the crossing.' Shrike was getting somewhere now. He could sense it. Corus was listening to him.

'No. We take the other route.'

'Past the garrison?' said Kadus.

'We pass unseen,' said Corus, by way of explanation.

'Sergeant...' started Shrike, before Kadus interjected.

'Yes, sergeant,' he said. His expression was hidden by his helm.

'Then I shall gather the others,' said Corus. He turned and walked away, his boots stirring the chalky dust.

Shrike started after him, but felt a restraining hand on his arm, and stopped. 'Let him go, brother. You've won one fight today. You won't win another.'

'Very well,' said Shrike. 'But if you're right, I've just convinced him to trade one bad decision for another.'

The ork garrison was more of an outlying guard post than any real fortified structure or bastion. The truth of the matter, Shrike knew, was that the orks had no need to fortify any of the old human city – the Astra Militarum had been confidently rebutted, and any surviving humans who might be eking out a living in the ruins posed little or no threat to their conquerors. The guard post was most likely there more as a watch-tower, observing the skies for any sign of Imperial activity. This close to the ork command post they'd be arming anti-aircraft weapons, with a view to eradicating any vessels that might sweep in to chance a bombing run.

From their observation point, it was impossible to tell if the structure had once served a different purpose, although Shrike suspected that beneath the ramshackle walls of beaten steel and brass, decorated with yet more of the odious glyphs, there was the skeleton of a human building. It resembled a tower, constructed over three levels, although the sense of symmetry and proportion were entirely wrong, resulting in something that looked as alien to Shrike as the greenskins themselves.

As Aarvus and Gradus' earlier reconnaissance had reported, the place was swarming with orks. Shrike had counted at least thirty of them, and suspected the true number to be at least double that, given the size of the building. It stood in an area of formal gardens, such as those that might surround a palace or governor's office, and seemed utterly incongruous in the midst of such finery. Sculpted bushes that had once resembled sleeping lions, but which had now been hacked up and despoiled by the orks, flanked the stately entrance.

Two orks, armed with stubby automatic rifles, stood guard, while others walked the ramparts above. Others still milled around without obvious aim, making the most of the opportunity to taunt one another with what were clearly intended to be obscene gestures. Some lay slumped against the barricades on the upper levels, snoring, while others struggled to count out ammunition shells, or sharpened blades against rasping whetstones.

The transmitter lay on the other side of the compound, about a mile away. They'd originally intended to give the garrison a wide berth, coming at the transmitter from behind, striking swiftly and pulling out before any of the orks had a chance to raise the alarm. Now, however, with the newly formed canyon at their backs, the only viable route – without crossing the gulf – was to pass close by the watch-tower. By cover of night, the Raven Guard would not have been troubled by such a prospect, but now, with the midday sun at its zenith and very little cover in between, Shrike had grave concerns. He knew he was not the only one.

'Sergeant, what do you propose?' This from Hirus, crouched behind the pedestal of a broken statue ahead of Shrike. 'Do we break cover one at a time, or do we go as one?'

Corus seemed to hesitate. 'One at a time. We reconvene on the other side of that tower.' Shrike risked a glance around the door-frame that served as his cover, spotting the tower in the distance. 'Do not engage the enemy. We cannot afford to find ourselves in the thick of another firefight. If the orks become aware of our presence, we scatter. Each of you has enough charges to blow the transmitter. Remember your mission.'

'Victorus aut mortis,' said Cavaan.

'Victorus aut mortis,' echoed the others.

'Aarvus. You have point. When you see your chance, take it. We shall await your signal.'

'Aye, sergeant,' said Aarvus.

Shrike peered up at the watch-tower. There were too many orks. They seemed largely preoccupied, but nevertheless, the chances of avoiding detection were remote, even for those as well trained in subtlety as the Raven Guard.

He fingered the trigger of his bolt pistol. He intended to make it to that transmitter, and a handful of xenos were not about to stop him. He would do whatever needed to be done.

All eyes were on Aarvus. Shrike's hearts quickened as he saw his brother break cover, keeping low, bearing right to hug the shadows that slanted across the courtyard: lazy silhouettes of the watch-tower, flattened across the marble concourse. He ducked behind the base of a broken pillar, melding with the shadows until even Shrike found him difficult to discern. He appeared to be studying the upper ramparts, waiting for one of the orks to turn its back.

Shrike craned his neck, trying to get a visual. That was what he'd have to watch for: from below, the uppermost tier was a near blind spot, but from above the ork guards would have a perfect vantage.

He looked back to see that Aarvus was on the move again. He'd almost reached the other side of the courtyard now. A few more yards and he'd be able to duck behind a low wall and run the rest of the way to the safety of some nearby ruins.

Shrike felt a surge of pride as Aarvus reached the wall and flung himself over without looking back. One down, seven to go.

Moments later, Shrike caught a glimpse of light flicker from the ruins. It only lasted a split-second, and to anyone other than the Raven Guard awaiting Aarvus' signal, might just have been a glint of sunlight on a broken metal spur. Corus, however, read the signal for what it was, and signalled for the next of them – Hirus – to make his move.

Once again, Hirus paused for a while, biding his time. The moment stretched. Just when Shrike was starting to think that something was wrong, he shot out from behind a hunk of masonry, following the same route as Aarvus around the courtyard, and slid into position behind the pillar. Shrike watched him glance up at the ramparts, decide that it was safe to move on, and as swiftly as he'd set off, he was gone, over the wall and snaking his way to safety.

This time Corus didn't wait for the signal, but gave the order for Arkus to follow. The pattern repeated itself. First Arkus, then Cavaan, then Gradus.

'I'll go next,' said Corus, his voice barely above a whisper. 'Then Shrike, then Kadus. Once we're over the other side, we'll neutralise the transmitter.'

Shrike nodded. He glanced over his shoulder to see Kadus crouched behind him, implacable as ever.

Corus crept along the length of fallen pillar he'd been using as cover, nestling in the shadows. His head turned fractionally, observing the orks above. Shrike counted six heartbeats before Corus moved, swerving right, following the path marked out by Aarvus. He dipped behind the pillar, and then lurched out again, heading for the wall.

Immediately, Shrike knew that something was

wrong. Corus had broken the pattern. He hadn't looked up to the ramparts, hadn't checked to see if there were any passing guards who might observe his final dash across the courtyard.

Shrike heard a cry, and risked a momentary glance to see one of the orks above readying its weapon, taking aim over the ramparts. With a bellow it cut loose, automatic rounds showering the marble concourse and sending bursts of chippings flying wildly in all directions.

Corus, winged by one of the rounds, returned fire with his bolt pistol, dropping two of the orks, before diving for the wall, throwing himself bodily onto the ground, just as more of the orks appeared on the ramparts, and the guards below raised their weapons, anxious to join the hunt.

Shrike sensed Kadus shifting position, and turned to see him raising his bolt pistol, looking for a clean shot at one of the guards.

'No!' hissed Shrike, reaching out a hand and forcing the end of Kadus' weapon down. 'Corus told us to scatter. So we scatter. Remember the mission. The others will get to the transmitter. We can regroup with Corus later.'

As he said the words, Shrike sensed that something was wrong. He turned, following Kadus' gaze, to see Corus on his feet, making a run for the ruins, heading directly for the location of Aarvus and the others.

The orks were chewing up the loam around Corus' boots as he ran, and Shrike could see that he was injured – he'd adopted a stumbling gait, caused by a wound to one leg, and one of his arms was hanging limp by his side.

'What is he *doing*?' said Kadus. 'He's putting the whole mission at risk.'

There was a whistling hiss from overhead, and Shrike looked up to see two orks on the ramparts, straining beneath the burden of an enormous rocket tube – a launcher that they had just aimed and fired in the direction of the sergeant.

With a sense of impending dread, Shrike watched as the ruins exploded in a vicious roar of light. The launcher was a primitive weapon, but no one could doubt its effectiveness. Flames licked at the dry earth, and even the surviving masonry, which had so far withstood the devastation of the seismic weapon and any number of previous conflagrations, dripped like molten lava, such was the ferocity of the heat.

As the orks above whooped in delight, Shrike and Kadus watched the ruins burn – and with it, any hope that their brothers had survived.

'It's over,' said Kadus. 'Nobody could have survived that.'

'It's *not* over,' said Shrike. 'We're still alive. Whatever's happened to the others, we still have our mission.'

Kadus sighed. 'Corus signed their death warrant, the moment he raised the alarm. All of them. Even if we blow the transmitter now, the orks know we're here. There's no way the two of us can bring down that entire garrison before one of them raises the alarm. They'll dig in and send for reinforcements. Saak's walking into a trap. It'll be a massacre.'

'Not necessarily,' said Shrike. 'If we can find a way to distract them for long enough, maybe we can reach the transmitter before they're able to report in.'

'You seem to be forgetting our present situation. If those orks on the ramparts get even a sense that there are more of us down here, they'll turn more heavy guns on our position. You've seen what that launcher can do.'

Shrike nodded. He knew that Kadus was as anxious as he was to see things through to the end. He wasn't fearful of death – only failure. 'How many grenades have you got left?'

Kadus checked the pouch at his belt. 'Four,' he said.

'Likewise. So we can spare two to cause a little disruption.' He weighed one of them in his palm.

'Shrike, are you sure about this?'

'The only thing I'm sure of, Kadus, is my duty. I cannot stand by and watch our mission fail. I will not allow Shadow Captain Saak and the others to walk to their death, and know that I did *nothing*. Nor will I allow Gorkrusha to deploy his seismic weapon on another Imperial world. Not while I'm still breathing.'

'Then I am with you, brother,' said Kadus. He reached into his pouch and withdrew a grenade. 'What is your plan?'

Shrike glanced at the watch-tower. 'Up there on the

ramparts. There are ammo caches beside those gun emplacements. We can set off a chain reaction and take out the entire upper level. The orks will think they are under siege, maybe even that Corus and some of the others have survived. By the time they've finished searching the grounds, we'll be long gone.'

'You mean to attempt a crossing of the courtyard during the confusion?'

'No. I mean to retreat to the canyon and use my jump pack to get to the other side.'

For a moment, Shrike thought that Kadus was about to object, and then he gave a short, sharp nod of agreement. 'I'll take the one on the left,' he said.

'Agreed. On my count…' Shrike thumbed the detonator. 'One, two, three, *now*!'

The two Space Marines lobbed their charges, ducking back into cover as the grenades sailed through the air.

The first to strike – thrown by Kadus – landed amongst the ammo cache itself, failing to even draw a glance from the attendant gunner, who seemed more interested in picking something from between his teeth with the end of a large knife. Shrike's struck the ground near the other gunner's feet with a metallic clunk, rolling until it came to rest by the creature's boots. It looked down, curious, just as the device detonated and vaporised the lower half of its body. The other exploded a second later, igniting the cache of explosive rounds, which erupted into a stuttering ball of flame that swallowed the entire upper gantry.

Burning bodies plummeted from the upper level, thudding into the plascrete below, while the entire watch-tower erupted in chaos. Automatic fire ricocheted off the marble courtyard as the orks opened fire indiscriminately, showering the grounds with bullets. Others were calling out in their strange, guttural language, barking commands, and hurriedly sending out small patrols to search the grounds for their attackers.

Shrike looked to Kadus and jabbed his finger in the opposite direction. Kadus nodded, and together they crept away from the looming shadow of the watch-tower, and the rest of their squad, whom they could only suppose were lost.

Shrike and Kadus stood at the edge of the canyon, which yawned before them, a brutal, savage scar in the very fabric of the world.

'We can burn out our jump packs,' said Shrike. 'Empty the tanks. That way we can get enough height and fall the rest of the way to the ledge. The chalk is pliable enough to climb once we're over.'

'It means we'll have to finish the mission on foot,' said Kadus.

'So be it,' said Shrike.

'Very well. But you're going first, since it's your idea.'

Shrike laughed, for the first time in days. He extended his arm, and the two of them clasped forearms. 'See you on the other side, brother.'

'One way or another,' said Kadus.

Shrike knew that Kadus was right. He was taking a risk – and the chance of success was minimal. Nevertheless, it had to be done. Now was not the time for doubts. He turned and walked a little further down the road, giving himself a clear run at the edge of the canyon. 'For Corax,' he said, 'and lost brothers.'

He drew a slow and deliberate breath, and then, dropping his head and shoulders, charged towards his fate.

He barrelled towards the lip of the canyon, his feet pounding the rockcrete, his hearts echoing their steady, rhythmic beat. Adrenaline surged in his system, and he felt more awake, more alive than he had since Kiavahr. Since that fateful day of the hunt.

His boot crunched on the loose stone of the canyon edge, and he triggered his jump pack to maximum burn, launching himself out over the void. The downward pressure of the jump pack lifted him high, and he soared, arms folded by his sides as he flew, urging himself on across the cavernous drop.

Ahead, he could see the ledge, a small, jutting promontory, formed during the seismic chaos caused by the ork weapon. He could feel his trajectory tailing off, the wind rushing past his helm as he dipped, his glide now turning slowly into a freefall. His jump pack was sputtering, the fuel canisters almost empty.

He wasn't going to make it. He was going to fall short, miss the ledge and tumble to his death at the bottom of the crevasse. There was nothing he could do. He was in the hands of fate, now, and it would do with him what it would.

He felt a sudden kick at his back as his jump pack shoved him forwards, and then the ground was suddenly coming up to meet him. Without thinking, he buried his head in the crook of his elbow and braced himself for impact. He struck the chalk ledge with enough force to carve a channel in its brittle surface, and to jar his power armour so brutally that seventeen impact alarms flared. He felt pressure escaping from a tear in one knee.

He rolled, dazed, until he slammed against the cliff-face, and only remembered to kill the thrust on his jump pack when he started sliding across the ground, heading for the edge of the ledge.

He came to rest only inches from the drop. He lay there for a moment, waiting for the pain to flare. To his surprise, it didn't. He glanced at each of the warning sigils in turn, checking for any material damage. One of his vambraces was weakened and his damaged shoulder pauldron would not survive a direct strike from an enemy round. His jump pack was as good as spent. Otherwise, he was alive.

He stood, looking back at the immensity of the crevasse he had just traversed. Kadus was standing on the far edge, staring down at him.

Shrike saw Kadus – now only a tiny silhouette – fling himself over the edge of the chasm, spreading his arms wide like a raven's wings. He soared through the air, his jump pack flaring, and Shrike watched as his brother seemed to float, drifting in slow motion, growing slowly larger and larger, until he was all that Shrike could see. He was falling now, and his jump pack spat, one of its thrusters stuttering out and sending him into a wild spin. He flung his arms forwards, reaching for the ledge, but it was clear he was going to miss it by no more than a few inches.

'Kadus!' Shrike had no time to consider his options. He ran to the end of the ledge and powered what was left of his own jump pack, leaping into the air and grasping hold of Kadus' wheeling arm. He cut the power, falling again, landing with his boots half on the edge of the ledge, and slipping backwards, falling, pulled down by the weight of his brother.

Shrike threw his left arm out, still clutching Kadus with the other, so that his fingers slammed into the chalky crust of the ledge. He dug them in, forcing them down through the brittle surface, slowing their descent, until the two of them were hanging over the abyss, held up by nothing more than Shrike's finger-tips.

'Use your jump pack,' called Shrike.

'It's dead,' said Kadus.

'Then I'll swing you up,' said Shrike, struggling to speak with the strain. He could feel his fingers slipping, his wrist about to give way. His shoulder burned, too, the wound rending open again, flesh and muscle popping as the ligaments tore. Fresh blood surged down his back and arm. 'Catch hold of the ledge and pull yourself up.'

'All right,' said Kadus.

With a roar of pain, Shrike flexed his arm, inching it back and forth as he worked up momentum, causing the dangling Kadus to swing precariously back and forth in his grasp. His fingers were beginning to slip on Kadus' vambrace, and he knew they only had moments left.

Kadus twisted in his grip, raising his own left arm, reaching for the lip... But his fingers closed on nothing, and he fell limp again, still swinging. 'Do it!' bellowed Kadus. 'Now!'

The words were like fire to Shrike, burning through his pain and weariness. He forced his fingers deeper into the chalk, and then, grunting, he started to swing Kadus back and forth again, this time allowing his entire shoulder to dislocate from its socket. With a final wrench, he heaved Kadus up and round.

This time, Kadus was able to catch hold of the ledge, pulling himself up. 'All right, let go. I've got it,' he said, and Shrike did as he requested, allowing his damaged arm to go limp.

Above, Kadus scrambled onto the ledge.

Blackness was threatening to close in on Shrike again. He felt his grip on the ledge loosening, and his fingers finally slipped from their hold. He slid back, tumbling away into the void.

Shrike awoke with a start.

For a moment he thought he was still falling, and wheeled his arms, grasping for a handhold, before

Kadus caught hold of him to stop him flailing. 'Shrike? It's Kadus.'

Shrike stared at him, trying to process what had happened. He had no recollection other than the fall: the pain, the anger… and then losing his grip and sliding away into the darkness. 'I fell,' he said, as if that were enough.

'I caught you,' said Kadus. 'Least I could do, given the circumstances.'

Shrike laughed mirthlessly. 'I think we're all going to die here, Kadus, and if not here, somewhere like it, some blasted, beaten rock, a million miles from home.'

They were sitting beside one another on the ledge, their backs to the cliff edge.

'It's a long way from Kiavahr, I'll grant you that,' said Kadus.

'I'd like to see it again,' said Shrike. 'At least once. I'd like to return these to the soil, to honour those who have fallen.' He grabbed the tiny bundle of skulls at his belt, and held them up, allowing them to cascade through his fingers.

'Aye, and to honour Corus and the others, too. They deserve that much,' said Kadus.

Shrike shifted, and winced at the lancing pain in his arm. 'Help me get this armour off,' he said.

Kadus cocked his head. 'We don't have time for that. You've been out for over ten minutes. We need to move, now, if we're ever going to blow that transmitter.'

Shrike shook his head. 'My shoulder is dislocated. I need to set it before I can climb.'

'You'd better hurry, then,' said Kadus. He stood, grabbing at Shrike's pauldron. Shrike stood motionless as Kadus hurriedly stripped his arm, unclamping the vambrace, sliding off the gauntlet. When he saw the state of Shrike's damaged shoulder, Kadus stared at him for a moment, as if in admiration.

'This shoulder's a mess,' he said. 'You'll be lucky to keep the arm.'

Shrike shrugged. 'As I said, we're probably going to die here anyway, so as long as it gets me out of this hole...'

Shrike grabbed the shoulder with his other hand and manipulated the joint back and forth, getting a measure of the damage. Then, gritting his teeth, he shoved it back into its socket. He flexed the joint. The muscles were stretched and torn, and Kadus was right – there was a chance he'd lose the limb entirely if it didn't receive attention soon. But it would last long enough for him to climb out of the crevasse, and hopefully long enough to see the mission through.

Kadus passed him his gauntlet. 'Come on, we've got work to do.'

Shrike clipped himself back into his power armour, as Kadus surveyed the cliff-face. There was around fifty yards left to climb and then, finally, they would be en route to their goal.

* * *

The climb was arduous, but the route back to the surface proved obvious, and the chalk pliant enough that the two Space Marines were able to scale it within minutes, despite their bulk. They emerged into a waning afternoon light, and to the distant report of gunfire. Shrike presumed it was the orks from the watch-tower still on the prowl, searching for further sign of their attackers. By now they'd have no doubt located the bodies of Corus and the others – or what was left of them – and established the nature of their black-armoured assailants. He hoped their diversion had been enough – they'd lost too much time crossing the canyon, not to mention the valuable minutes they'd wasted in the grounds of the watch-tower earlier.

Corus had been wrong, and he'd paid for his mistake with his life. Unfortunately, so had Aarvus, Gradus and the others. The thought left a bitter aftertaste in Shrike's mouth. Now, those brothers were lost, their gene-seed gone. It was unlikely their corvia would be recovered, either, nor that of the longer dead they carried on their belts. They would be cheated of their right to be honoured in the forests of Kiavahr, instead remembered *in absentia* – their totems left to burn on a distant world awaiting Exterminatus.

Shrike couldn't help but feel responsible. He'd urged Corus to press on with the mission, despite the danger. And then there was Kiavahr, and all that had happened there, so long ago.

He shook his head. There would be time for guilt and recriminations later. Others were relying upon him now.

Kadus was studying the read-out of his auspex. 'If we stick to the original route, the road ahead should curve to the west. There's a path through the ruins, and then we reach the final communications array.'

They set out, hugging the shadows, running with a speed that belied their fatigue and injuries. At all times they remained alert, watchful for any clue that patrols, or any enemy scavengers, were picking amongst the wreckage. Shrike had heard tales of looters, bands of wandering orks who searched the human ruins for any technology or weapons they could repurpose, turning them into twisted parodies – war machines like the one he'd seen earlier amongst the ruins of the Astra Militarum vehicles. The pickings here were rich, at least in the sectors that had not already been hit by the quakes.

The city remained a tomb, however, abandoned by those who had lived and fought there, and left to rot and ruin by those who had deposed them.

It was almost two miles later when they first registered another sign of life.

'Hold,' said Kadus. 'There's something up ahead.'

They slowed, creeping into the long shadows of a ditch that ran parallel to the road.

Shrike peered into the dimness ahead, using the display inside his helm to supplement his natural vision. 'They're not orks. Too small.'

'No,' said Kadus. 'I think...' He activated his vox. 'Sergeant?' he said, tentatively. 'Sergeant Corus?'

Up ahead, the two figures stopped. 'Kadus?' came the weary response, cloaked in crackling interference. 'Where are you, brother?'

Shrike looked across at Kadus in disbelief. Although he could not see his brother's expression, he sensed that Kadus, too, had been taken aback by the revelation.

Corus was still alive, along with another of their squad.

Shrike put a hand on Kadus' shoulder. 'Proceed with caution, brother. Ork eyes are everywhere.'

Kadus nodded, and then continued his brisk run through the ditch. Shrike followed behind, keeping a watchful eye on the surrounding ruins.

Corus, when they reached him, was not in a good way. He was leaning heavily upon Cavaan, the entire left side of his body ravaged by the explosion. The ceramite of his armour had melted, melding with his pale flesh, which itself had blistered and bubbled, weeping openly with blood and other, unidentifiable fluids. He'd removed his beaked helm and his face, too, was scarred, his mouth drooping, the lips almost entirely burned away. His left eye was nothing but a vacant, staring hole. His breathing was laboured, his power armour too damaged to sustain him. He was dying, that much was immediately evident. Shrike couldn't help but think that he'd be better off if one of them put their bolt pistol to his head and put him out of his misery. He knew it might yet come to that.

Cavaan, on the other hand, appeared entirely undamaged, save for the injury he had sustained in their earlier roadside battle. 'Brothers,' he said, as they approached. 'It is good to see you.'

'Likewise,' said Shrike, still wary of ork trickery. 'We presumed you dead.'

'For a while I was certain that I was. When the orks opened fire and the ruins exploded, I was sure that none of us would survive. I saw Gradus lose his head, caught in the blast wave. Aarvus roasted alive inside his armour. Hirus cast to the four winds in fragments no bigger than your fist. The sergeant, too, flung back by the force of the explosion, his armour glowing red-hot with the ferocity of the flames.' Despite Cavaan's best efforts to remain detached, Shrike could hear the tremble of regret in his voice.

'How, then, brother, did you survive unscathed?' said Kadus.

'Luck,' said Cavaan. 'I'd taken cover inside a small side-chamber in the ruins, with a view over the court-yard. The blast brought the roof down, burying me under a pile of rubble.' He turned, showing them his back, and Shrike saw for the first time that his armour there was pitted and dented, his jump pack cracked and fizzing with sparking electrics.

'I remained conscious while the ork patrols passed through. The crunch of every boot upon the gravel brought the certainty of death, but I soon realised that the fallen masonry had hidden me from detection. I waited until the patrols had all passed, and then dug my way out.'

'And the sergeant?' said Shrike, glancing at Corus.

'The orks had left him for dead,' said Cavaan. 'I searched for our brothers amongst the wreckage, but found only enough of their remains to claim the corvia of Gradus and Arkus. When I tried to do the same for the sergeant, I realised he was still breathing.'

Cavaan looked from Shrike to Kadus. 'I knew we had to finish the mission. I hoped you'd got away, but knew that coming after you was folly. The courtyard was alive with the enemy, and with the sergeant injured, we risked drawing attention to ourselves, and worse, to you. We continued through the ruins, avoiding the ork patrols, until we emerged close to here.'

Kadus nodded. 'Then we continue. We are close to the final transmitter.' He looked to Shrike. 'But the sergeant will slow us down, and time is also our enemy.'

'You cannot take me with you, if you hope to have any chance,' said Corus, his voice a wet, rasping, croak.

'I shall remain with him,' said Cavaan, 'until you return.'

'No,' said Corus, releasing his hold on Cavaan, pushing him away. 'I'm already dead. You must see that. I won't make it back to the rendezvous, and there's no evacuation coming.'

'But sergeant...' said Cavaan.

'Let him go,' said Shrike. He crossed to Corus, aiding his unsteady progress to the roadside. Shrike lowered him down, until he was resting in a sitting position, and Shrike was crouched over him.

'I'm sorry,' said Corus, his voice weak. 'You must know that, Kayvaan. I never meant for this...' He trailed off, spluttering, blood trickling from the corner of his mouth. He didn't even have the strength to wipe it away.

'I know, Corus,' said Shrike. 'Kadus and I... We know.'

With his good arm, Corus reached down and yanked a solitary corvia from his belt, holding it out to Shrike, cradling it in his massive fist. It looked so small, yet signified so much. 'Take it,' he said. 'It's yours.'

'I will honour you, brother,' said Shrike, 'on distant Kiavahr. I shall set you free amongst the ravens, where your spirit will soar.'

'It's more than I deserve,' said Corus. He was fading now, and Shrike could see the awareness slipping from his eyes. He searched Corus' belt, locating his combat knife. He held it out so Corus could see. 'I'll return this, sergeant, once I've wet it with xenos blood.'

Corus gave a wet laugh. 'Keep it,' he said. His expression turned suddenly serious, his black eyes flitting across Shrike's helm, as if trying to focus. 'Do one last thing for me, Kayvaan.'

Shrike gave a slight nod of understanding. He stooped and plunged the blade into Corus' chest, puncturing his primary heart.

'For Corax,' said Shrike.

'Victorus aut mortis,' said Kadus, from behind him.

Shrike didn't look back as he broke into a run, the others falling in behind him, their footfalls barely making an impression in the sodden loam.

There were only nine orks patrolling the area around the third communications array. It was smaller than the two they'd previously destroyed, sited on a small hillock, and Shrike supposed that this deep in the heart of occupied territory, the greenskins were arrogant enough to believe they were not at risk of attack.

The transmitter consisted of a single mast, along with two powercells and a splayed web of antenna, opening like an inverted umbrella at the top of a central stem. Lights blinked as transmissions were collected, translated and fed out again to various points in the ork encampment.

There was no time for reconnaissance; if the guards were sitting atop a nest of reinforcements, then the Raven Guard would simply have to deal with the consequences. The only thing that mattered was blowing the array.

'We strike from the shadows,' said Shrike. 'Cavaan – circle the hillock and come at them from behind. Kadus, you take the left. I'll go in from the right. Swift and sure.'

Cavaan nodded, and set off at a run, sliding into the shadows and disappearing from sight.

'Emperor be with you, brother,' said Kadus. He turned and ran after Cavaan.

Shrike allowed the others a few more moments to get into position, watching the orks as they patrolled the edges of the array, and then moved. He ran up the side of the hillock, keeping to the slanting shadows, his armour barely making a sound.

He was three feet from the closest ork before it noticed him, and he didn't give it the opportunity to call out a warning. Its eyes widened as his blade ruptured its throat, slicing through tough, fibrous hide, through arteries and vocal cords. It gurgled, its hands going to the wound, as if trying to hold everything in, blood spraying out between its gnarly digits.

Shrike didn't bother to watch it die. He twisted, pistol arm coming up and loosing off two shots, taking out both eyes of a second ork. His chainsword ripped open its belly a moment later, spilling ropey intestines across the muddy ground.

He heard another chainsword roar to life to his left, and shots being fired over the other side of the hill, as he yanked his chainsword free of the creature's guts and jabbed it straight behind him, catching another ork – that had been attempting to sneak up behind him – in the groin. It howled in pain, falling back in shock, and he turned, forcing the chainsword up and out through its chest.

It slumped to the ground in a growing puddle of filth.

Cavaan was walking towards him, dripping in orkish blood. A quick glance told him that Kadus had nearly seen to the last of the orks, removing its head with a swipe of his burring chainsword.

He joined them a moment later. Shrike was already priming another krak grenade. 'Get clear,' he said. He walked to the transmitter, tossing the grenade into the coils of wiring at the base of the structure.

Together, the three Space Marines walked away down the hillside as the transmitter exploded with a blinding flash, electricity discharging from the ruptured powercells like bottled lightning trying to get back to the sky. In the waning light, the detonation would have been visible for miles.

Shrike's hearts were thrumming so hard that he could hear nothing but the roar of rushing blood, and the whistling of his ragged breath through the grille of his helm.

They'd given away their position, and probably given warning to a thousand orks that there were Imperial forces at work in their midst, but regardless, they'd done it. The greenskin communication network was finally down, and Shadow Captain Saak could make his move on the enemy command.

'Victory,' said Kadus, ducking behind the cover of a nearby doorway that, somehow, had remained relatively untouched by the war.

'No,' said Shrike. 'We've lost many of our brothers,

and the mission was too hard won. This does not feel like a victory.' He knew there would be questions to answer, back on the battle-barge – questions about Corus' command, and the choices that had been made. Questions too, perhaps, of Shrike himself, and his actions following their ill-fated attempt to circumnavigate the canyon.

For now, though, it was over. All that was left was to make it back to the rendezvous point for extraction.

'What is this place?' said Cavaan, from beside him, stirring him from his thoughts.

Shrike peered up at the towering doorway, with its concentric archways and moulded gargoyles. They peered down at him, their faces now worn and misshapen from centuries of wind and rain. With their impish wings and wolfish grins, they were a far cry from the real daemons he had fought on Indricas during the Seravixas campaign. 'An old Ecclesiarchy temple, I believe,' he said, 'although the Emperor only knows why it's still standing.' It might have just been the angle, but from outside, the whole building appeared relatively intact.

'It's probably been here for a thousand years,' said Kadus, 'or longer. In those days they built things to last.'

'I think it's older than that,' said Shrike. 'Can't you sense it? This place has been here for millennia.'

The door was a banded, wooden affair, at least five times the full height of Shrike, even in his armour.

He gave it a shove, and it creaked open on rusted hinges.

'Careful,' warned Kadus. 'The place could be swarming with orks.'

Shrike nodded, reaching for his weapon. Somehow, though, he had the sense that it wasn't. There was an air of something hallowed here, some eerie presence, and he wondered if it was this that had kept the orks away, perhaps in fear of supernatural reprisal against any that brought their desecration to this ancient place.

It was a grandiose edifice, built to the glory of the God-Emperor, and, as Shrike stepped over the threshold, his footsteps echoing in the dust-coated vestry, he felt overcome by a sense of pure awe. The vaulted ceiling, so high above his head that he had to crane his neck to see it, was decorated by a star map of the galaxy, the systems and constellations all filigreed in gold. He recognised Terra at the heart of it all, a shining beacon of hope, bringing light to all the many worlds of the Imperium. This map, he knew, was as old as the ancient Legions themselves, for it was only the work of moments to discern that the stars themselves had altered in the time since it was rendered. New worlds had been conquered, and others had been destroyed. This was a map from the ancient days, from before the Great Heresy, when even Corax himself was young.

Shrike walked along the central aisle, absorbing the aura of the place. Ornamental glass windows the size of hab-blocks lined the walls, each of them laying out a narrative from the ancient days, stories of the Great Crusade and the expansion of the Imperium across the stars. Here, heroes now lost to the mists of time raised their axes against strange, leviathan beasts, clashed swords with fleet-footed eldar, even stood toe-to-toe with hordes of greenskins, as they purged the galaxy of the alien menace.

At the rear of the building, an immense stone effigy of the Emperor Himself stood upon an engraved pedestal, flanked by twin lions, each roaring in defiance of His enemies. He was modelled in a pose of supplication, resting upon one knee, His head bowed, His sword tip buried in the earth, pommel extended as a gift to the pilgrim. This was the Emperor offering Himself up to His wards, the human race. This was the Emperor swearing His allegiance to mankind, as protector, overseer and champion.

Shrike stood beneath His watchful, unseeing gaze, and felt smaller than he had ever felt before. Had the Emperor witnessed his actions here on Shenkar, and judged him? Would he prove worthy? Shrike honestly didn't know.

Behind the Emperor, hanging like a tattered curtain upon the wall, was a tapestry. It had once been colourful, bordered in a deep crimson, but was now faded and threadbare, like a mirage witnessed in the heat of a desert, or a reflection in a pool of water, hazy and out of focus. Ragged holes had been chewed through the central image by rats, birds or other native fauna, and thick cobwebs obscured much of what survived. Nevertheless, Shrike could see it comprised a number of armoured figures, standing behind this towering statue of the Emperor, as if in servitude, lending Him their strength. These, Shrike knew, were His children, the primarchs of old, the founders of the Space Marine Legions. All were now lost to the annals of time.

Corax stood amidst his brothers, resplendent in his ebon armour, his lightning talons sparking with barely suppressed power. Shrike felt his hearts swell with pride. Here was the greatest warrior the Raven Guard had ever known, the founder of their Legion and the architect of everything Shrike held sacred. Shrike, Kadus and the others – each of them carried Corax's genetic legacy; but more than that, his code of honour, his sense of allegiance and his imperfections.

This was what he had given himself over to become a part of, all those years ago on Kiavahr. This was the legacy he had taken on, the burden he had proven himself worthy to bear during the trials of his initiation.

Shrike only hoped that he was still as worthy now.

A short burst of static hissed in his ear, and he turned, expecting to see Kadus calling him away from his reverie. Instead, he found both Kadus and Cavaan as lost amongst the grandeur of the ancient temple as he had been. He frowned, crossing to the door. There was no sign of movement amongst the scrubland or ruins.

The vox hissed again, and then he caught a snatch of a voice, almost lost amidst the chatter of bolter fire.

'...knew we were coming... so many... evacuate...'

It was Shadow Captain Saak, broadcasting on a long-range vox. Shrike turned to Kadus, who was staring at him from across the room. He'd heard it too.

'We were too late,' said Shrike, bunching his fist in frustration. 'As we suspected. The orks knew they were coming. They got a warning out.' He felt the rage welling up inside of him. Rage directed at the green-skins, at Corus, at himself.

He triggered his vox. 'Captain?' There was no response. 'Captain Saak, could you clarify your orders?'

There was nothing but the crackle of static in reply.

'We've sent them to their deaths,' said Kadus.

'It's worse than that,' said Shrike. 'If Gorkrusha is allowed to live, then we've just signed the death warrant of millions more. He cannot be allowed to deploy that weapon on another world.'

'I cannot see what we can do,' said Cavaan. 'There are only three of us. We have our orders. The captain said to evacuate. Even if we wished to lend him our strength, there are not enough of us to turn the tide of battle against the orks.'

Shrike considered this for a moment. He knew Cavaan was right – three more bolt pistols against a tide of greenskins would simply result in three more dead Raven Guard, when the final tally was taken. But perhaps there was another way... 'We may not be in a position to aid Captain Saak, but we can still complete his mission.'

'How so?' said Kadus.

'We do not allow their sacrifice to be in vain. None of them. We use them as a distraction. While the orks are engaged with our brothers, we infiltrate their command hub.'

'And do what?' said Kadus. 'Assassinate Gorkrusha? Take out his lieutenants? Kayvaan – you're wounded. Cavaan is wounded. How do you propose we take on the biggest and most ferocious orks in the invasion force?'

'I don't,' said Shrike. 'I'm proposing we turn their machine against them. This seismic weapon – whatever it is, however it works – the captain said it was controlled from that location in the cliff. What if we get inside and use it to bring the entire place down on their heads?'

'It's a suicide mission,' said Cavaan. 'We'd never get out.'

Shrike glanced at the statue of the Emperor. He seemed to be staring directly into Shrike's soul. 'Our duty isn't to survive. Our duty is to defend the Imperium from its enemies.'

'Our duty is to our captain,' said Kadus. 'He ordered us to evacuate.'

'Did he?' said Shrike. 'Was that an order? I asked

him to clarify, but received no response. If Saak were here, Kadus, what would he say?'

Kadus sighed. 'He'd tell you to do it.'

'Don't you think he would have considered that?' said Cavaan. 'The idea of turning the ork weapon against them.'

'Perhaps,' admitted Shrike. 'The plan was to infiltrate the base while the orks were unaware of us, to plant further charges inside the cliff, and then retreat, blowing the place wide open from a safe distance. If he met resistance on the doorstep, however, the entire squad will have been tied down in a firefight ever since.'

'A fight they can't possibly hope to win,' said Kadus. He put a hand on Shrike's pauldron. 'Are you sure of this path, brother?'

'I am sure of our intent, and I would willingly give my life to see it realised,' said Shrike.

'Then that shall have to do,' said Kadus. 'I stand with you.'

'As do I,' said Cavaan.

'Then we shall waste no more time,' said Shrike. He followed Kadus to the door. 'Swiftly, now. Think of nothing else but our goal.'

The twin suns had now slipped below the horizon, leaving only a silvery gloaming over the ruined city, and the distant glow of raging fires, under-lighting the clouds. The encroaching darkness would aid the Space Marines as they moved through territory that was likely crawling with the enemy. They were in their element now, swift and sure. They had purpose. They would use the orks' strength and arrogance against them, and they would put an end to Gorkru-sha and his reign of terror.

With a final glance back at the tapestry on the wall, Shrike closed the door to the Ecclesiarchy building and stepped out into the night.

The Raven Guard heard the fight before they saw it, like brooding, distant thunder, rumbling over the horizon. The landscape here was imposing, and the cliff-face loomed large and desolate on their left, a blank, pale monolith, dominating the skyline. Strange flying creatures with leathery wings, each the size of a man, circled their eyries high above, keeping an observant eye on the fighting below.

Shrike could see now that the city was, indeed, set within a vast bowl in the earth, as if an entire hunk of the planet had been scooped out to form a massive crater within which to build. It should have been easily fortified and defended by the Impe-rial forces, but the orks had smashed their way in, and their warlord, Gorkrusha, had erected his lair within these cliffs, digging in to the pliant chalk and hollowing out a warren. Now, Shrike would root him out from his hole, like a raven searching for a fresh worm.

He urged the others to stay back while he crept ahead, darting from cover to cover through the ruins. Too close, and he risked drawing the attention of the enemy combatants. Too far, and he'd be unable to discern the best point of entry into the warren.

He crouched behind a rumple of churned rock-crete, furled up by some weeks'-old explosion, and peered at the unfolding scene. In the distance he could see the muzzle flare of chattering bolters, and the excessive flash-bang of ork weapons as the xenos returned fire. The latter were contained within a small area at the foot of the cliff, near to a large void that Shrike assumed to be the main entrance to the cave system.

Above this, there were at least three smaller openings, chiselled into the cliff-face at various heights, in which other orks crouched, taking pot-shots at the Space Marines below.

He immediately ruled out the main entrance as a viable point of entry. They would need to cross the field of battle to even be in with a chance of getting close, and then the sheer number of orks gathered in the confined space would make it impossible to find a path inside that avoided detection.

The lowest of the smaller openings was about seventy feet up the chalk-face – a hole about the size of three orks, presumably opening up into the tunnel system they'd carved in the cliff behind. He had no way of mapping the interior structure of the warren. Once inside, they'd have to trust their instincts, working their way through the labyrinth in search of the control station that powered the seismic weapon.

The question was how to get up to the opening in

the first place, and how to deal with the orks that were squatting there, loosing off shots and hooting gleefully at every explosion.

Carefully, Shrike made his way back to the others. 'There's an entrance in the cliff-face up ahead. We'll have to scale the chalk to get in, but the orks are otherwise engaged, and the darkness is on our side.'

He led them through the wasteland to where he'd observed the battle a few moments earlier. 'Up there,' he said, gesturing at the cliff. 'Wait here and watch for my signal.'

He crept out from behind the cover of the shattered road, keeping low, moving unseen through the ork lines. The battlefield was a stuttering light show of vivid flares and deep shadows, the ground churned and muddy with spilt blood. He circled the corpse of a fallen ork, disturbed by its staring, soulless eyes and its ferocious visage, as if it had died in the throes of a bestial roar, and was continuing it after death by force of will alone.

Out in the darkness he could hear the burr of engines, and a quick glance identified the beams of headlamps, bouncing over the rough earth. The orks had deployed vehicles now, it seemed, armed with heavy stubber turrets that droned noisily like buzzing insects.

It seemed Shadow Captain Saak was giving the orks plenty to worry about.

Up ahead, the orks were beginning to fan out from the shelter of the main entrance, growing bolder, either from sheer arrogance, or from a thirst for battle. Either way, it made his present task harder, but would help when it came to making the ascent into the warren.

He froze as an ork turned its gaze in his direction, affecting a position of utter stillness, his ebon-armour becoming one with the shadows. Apparently seeing nothing of interest, the ork turned its head towards the battle in search of more engaging diversions.

A few more steps saw Shrike splashing through a muddy ditch, and then he was there, at the foot of the cliff, looking up at his target. He pressed himself against the chalk, surveying his surroundings. There was little or no cover to be found, aside from the waterlogged ditch, which might prove useful if his next action drew any unwanted attention.

He took three steps back, carefully selecting his angle, and then, thumbing the detonator, tossed a krak grenade up into the tunnel entrance.

He heard a bellow of surprise, and then the cave mouth lit up in a flare of light and heat.

The boom from the explosion was deafening, amplified by the confined space in the tunnel mouth. Secondary detonations continued to sound for a full minute afterwards as the ammunition in the orks' weapons also went up, showering burning fragments on the creatures below like fiery hail. Shrike stayed close to the wall, blending with the shadows.

As he had predicted, the orks on the ground paid little heed to the chaos occurring above, remaining focused on the more tangible threat before them. They must have assumed it was simply a successful strike from Saak's forces on the ground – although Shrike was wary of accrediting most of them with that much intelligence; for the most part, the orks appeared to be thick-skulled brutes, and all the more dangerous because of it.

Shrike glanced back to where he'd left Cavaan and Kadus. He could see nothing but darkness, but he knew they were there, watching for him. He gave the sign for them to join him, and saw two black shadows detach from the others and slide across the road, disappearing for a moment amongst the debris littering the battlefield.

Shrike crossed to the foot of the cliff again, dripping with foul water. He slipped Corus' combat knife back into the sheath on his leg, and searched the cliff-face for any foot and handholds. They were few and far between. They'd have to make their own.

He sensed movement and turned to see two black-clad figures emerging from the gloaming behind him. He made a gesture, telling them to remain silent, and then pointed up to the opening in the cliff, where the remains of an ork were still slumped and burning, hanging half out of the tunnel mouth.

Slowly, Shrike worked a handhold in the chalk with his fingers and hauled himself up. Another followed, and soon he was half way to the tunnel mouth, always remaining in the shadows, freezing whenever an explosion cast a flicker of light over the cliff. Behind him, first Cavaan, then Kadus made the ascent, following in Shrike's wake.

A moment later, and Shrike was heaving himself over the lip of the hole and into the tunnel itself. The place stank of seared flesh and cordite. The chalk here was roughly hewn and blackened by the explosion, marred by pockmarks caused by the detonating ammunition. The four orks who'd been crouched in the tunnel were now little more than burned husks, ribcages poking through the twisted remains of their armour, cooked alive in the confined space and unable to escape. One had lost its head completely, the ragged stump cauterised by the blast that had taken it.

Shrike found it a few steps further down the passageway, where it had rolled to a halt against the wall, trailing broken spinal column. He sidestepped it, peering further along the tunnel. There didn't appear to be any more orks in the vicinity, and he heard no sign of any en route.

He looked back to see Kadus and Cavaan clambering over the still smouldering remains of the orks. He activated his vox.

'Avoid engaging the enemy. If it cannot be avoided, disable them swiftly with your combat knife. Only fire your bolt pistol if it will further the mission. Agreed?'

'Aye,' murmured Kadus and Cavaan in concert.

'Act swiftly,' said Shrike. 'We cannot cover our tracks or secure egress.' He drew Corus' blade, and gestured for the others to follow behind him.

The tunnel narrowed up ahead, before making a sudden turn to the right, worming deeper into the cliff. He detected a gradient here, the floor gradually sloping away, leading them down into the caverns at the heart of the warren.

Gorkrusha had built himself an eminently defendable position from which to oversee his campaign on Shenkar – a labyrinth in which even the Raven Guard were at a grave disadvantage. The orks knew the tunnels here, and Shrike could see now that even if Saak had managed to breach their defences, he'd have certainly failed in his goal.

Shrike paused at the junction, peered around the corner and battle-signed to the others. They crept in single file, Shrike first, followed by Cavaan and then Kadus.

It was clear now that these tunnels were intended only to provide vantage points for the ork guards; no rooms or branching passageways had been carved out of the chalk this high in the cliff. Shrike couldn't help but feel he was being drawn in, shepherded by the structure itself towards whatever awaited him at the heart of the warren.

They reached their first branching point a short while later, and Shrike reasoned that the other tunnel would wind back up into the cliff, providing access to one of the higher vantage points he'd seen from the battlefield below. His instincts told him to keep moving lower, deeper into the ork hold.

Their first sign of trouble was the low grunt of ork

voices, coming from the passageway directly ahead. Here, the corridor widened into what appeared to be a small chamber, and Shrike sent Cavaan ahead to make a quick reconnaissance.

Cavaan edged closer, clutching his combat knife in his fist, ready to strike if he was discovered. He reached the chamber mouth and craned his neck, so that the beak of his helm emerged only momentarily into the room, before withdrawing and edging a little way back into the passage. He made a series of gestures to Shrike and Kadus.

Two orks, one exit.

They were going to have to take them out.

Shrike nodded and crept along the passage to join him. He signalled his plan to the others. He would enter the room, circle round and take out one of the orks, while the two of them moved in and took the other. They had to be swift. If either of the orks managed to bark out a warning, their whole mission was in jeopardy.

He held up his fist, and then dropped it, signalling them to go.

The Space Marines moved in a sudden blur. Shrike whirled into the room, moving around behind the smaller of the two greenskins and jabbing his combat blade straight into its exposed throat. His first cut severed its vocal cords; the second opened its jugular in a wide smile. He felt the creature buck in his arms as he grappled with it, containing its death throes, and then it slumped to the floor in a growing pool of its own blood.

He looked up to see Cavaan standing over the corpse of the other ork, its head nearly separated from its neck. He was dripping with gore, his blade still clutched in his bloodied fist. The ork had not died well, but Cavaan had seen to it that the creature had been silenced.

Shrike wiped his own blade on the dead ork's arm, and then sheathed it.

The chamber was clearly an ammunitions dump – the walls were lined with racks of shells and mismatched ork weapons, some of them salvaged from the Imperial forces they'd defeated.

It was clear they were getting closer to the heart of the ork stronghold, now. The passageways were widening and other, smaller corridors branched off into a series of antechambers. These were used, Shrike guessed, as temporary barracks for the guards.

Mercifully, the rooms were largely unoccupied, with most of the orks engaged in fighting Saak's forces outside. Those that did contain occupants were ignored, with Shrike and the others whispering past, silent and intent.

Ahead, the main tunnel merged with another, which dropped at a steeper incline, and Shrike realised that they had now dipped below ground level. Soon these tunnels would collapse beneath the ferocity of the orks' own weapon, and Gorkrusha's advance into Imperial space would be quashed.

The distant whirr of machinery – accompanied by the rhythmic thump-thump of firing pistons – informed

Shrike that the control room was close by. As they moved further down the incline, the noise grew louder, masking the sound of their own passing, but in turn making it harder to discern the presence of orks.

They pressed on. The lighting here was dim, provided only by lanterns strung at irregular intervals upon electric cable dangling from the ceiling. They cast a warm, amber glow against the dirty white chalk, and it suddenly occurred to Shrike that Phaeros' squad, too, must have failed – the bunker was still drawing power from somewhere. He wondered what had become of the others, and whether any of them had survived. He supposed he'd never know.

The thumping of the machine had now reached a crescendo, and Shrike gestured to the others to take up guard positions as he crept to the end of the passageway. Here, the tunnel made a dogleg to the right, continuing on into the depths of the cliff. On the left, however, it branched off into a large cavern. Shrike could only just see inside, but it was immediately clear that this was where the quake machine was housed – he could see two gaudily painted pistons firing in continuous succession, driving two massive steel arms into shafts in the ground.

He could also see there were orks in the room – at least five of them, two armed with massive guns, the others clambering over the equipment, wielding wrenches and oil cans. He suspected there were others, too, out of his line of sight.

He crept back to where the others were waiting, their combat knives drawn and ready.

'Around the corner on the left,' he whispered, his voice barely audible over the thump of the machine. 'That's our goal. The place is guarded by xenos. Take them out quickly so we can get at the machine.'

'For Corax!' said Kadus

'For Corax!' echoed Cavaan.

Together, they crept to the end of the passageway. The only sound was the continued hammering of the machine, thrashing out its song of lament.

Shrike gave the signal, and the three Space Marines burst into the room, bolt pistols flaring as they let loose on the guards. Two of the orks, caught suddenly unaware, howled in pain as they dropped, while the others returned fire, hot plasma spurting from the glowing mouths of their weapons.

Shrike kept his back to the wall, muzzle flare under-lighting his beaked helm. He hunched his shoulders, tracking the movements of the enemy, twisting from the waist as he targeted first one, then another, then a third. His armour was pitted and dripping with scolding plasma, but he continued to pace around the edges of the room, felling ork after ork, while his brothers did the same.

Orks were now emerging from the tunnels behind them, appearing in the doorway, and Cavaan turned his attention to them, driving them back, his chainsword roaring as he ran at them, disappearing into the tunnel beyond as he fought to keep them at bay.

Shrike glanced across at Kadus, who was butchering another ork with his combat knife, gouging its throat, the gash so deep that the head remained connected by only a thin strip of flesh. The noise of the skirmish made it almost impossible to think – ricochets pinging off the walls, floor and ceiling, blood spray bright and satisfying against the stark white chalk. It was working, though – aside from the orks that Cavaan had driven back into the tunnels beyond, there were only two of them left.

Shrike launched himself at one, ignoring the plasma bolt that seared his chest-plate. His chainsword ruptured its face and cut deep into the skull, turning its brains to pulp. He swung his other arm out, taking snap shots at the remaining ork, but Kadus beat him to it, punching holes in its chest with his pistol, fired at point-blank range.

The final corpse dropped to the floor, and for a moment the two of them – Shrike and Kadus – stood at the centre of the room, dripping in gore. In the tunnels outside, the echoes of Cavaan's pistol were still ringing loudly as he continued to drive the other orks back.

Kadus quickly checked the bodies of the engineers for signs of life. They were slumped where they had fallen, oozing blood and effluvia. One of them, draped across a counterweight that swung pendulously beneath its bulk, was still breathing, and Kadus finished it with a shot to the head. It slid unceremoniously to the ground, its skull casing blown and brain matter seeping into the chalky dust.

The machine, Shrike could now see, was of primitive construction, but capable of deploying incredible force. The ground around the mechanism trembled as the hammers lifted and fell, striking deep beneath the earth and sending tremors rippling out into the wider city. Winking sensors lined the opening of each shaft, and hoards of unfamiliar components glimmered amongst coils of wire. He recognised the markings of the Adeptus Mechanicus impressed into the casing of some, while others seemed of cruder, alien design.

One of the dead orks had crashed into what Shrike took to be the control station. He crossed to it, heaving the body onto the ground and examining the panel of buttons and levers. The machine was currently operational. All he had to do was alter the target coordinates to centre on their present location. He cranked one of the levers experimentally and the pistons sped up, slamming their payload into the earth with even more violence than before. He left the machine running at full capacity, assuming it would only help to hasten the collapse of the tunnel system.

Beside the lever was a hololithic dataslate, clearly salvaged from one of the Astra Militarum vehicles and crudely wired into the terminal. It appeared to have been stripped from a targeting control system, and while Shrike wasn't entirely familiar with how it operated, it didn't take him long to fathom how to input a set of coordinates.

He thumbed through the display on the slate. A few gestures later and the coordinates had been altered. The machine made a grinding sound as the arms contracted, and then the thumping started again, this time far louder, and directly underfoot. Shrike felt the entire cliff tremble around him.

Without hesitation he grabbed his bolt pistol and opened fire on the terminal until the dataslate was nothing but a steaming pile of slag.

He felt Kadus' hand upon his pauldron, urging him to go.

The walls were already shaking violently, and chalk dust was stirring, the hastily dug tunnels creaking beneath the weight of the mountain. Soon the whole place would collapse, and the machine would be destroyed. The mountain would swallow them, as if they had never been there at all.

Shrike followed Kadus out of the cavern at a run, turning right and mounting the slope that would lead them back to ground level.

He saw Kadus hesitate for a moment at the top of the slope, and guessed he had caught sight of some fleeing orks, attempting to evacuate the hold before the roof came down. But then he saw the shadow upon the wall, lumbering towards them; it was just one ork, but this was no normal greenskin.

The ork that stepped into their path was at least twice the size of the others, so big that it had to hunker down to fit within the confines of the tunnel. Its green flesh was scarred and puckered from scores of ancient wounds, and it wore a shoulder brace adorned with yellowed tusks that might have once been the teeth of its rivals.

A glowing red lens had replaced its left eye, and wires spilled from the device, looping around the back of its head and entering the skull cavity behind its ear. Its lower jaw had been enhanced by vicious-looking iron teeth, bolted into the bone with fat rivets. Likewise, its right arm had gone, replaced by a mechanical counterpart that terminated in a massive, whirring drill.

A partial exoskeleton, powered by twin pistons, encased its legs and waist, lending it extra strength, and from its belt hung a battered metal plate, shaped to resemble the glyph that Shrike had seen daubed across the wreckage of the city.

In its left hand it carried Cavaan by the throat, swinging him like a lifeless puppet. It peered at Shrike for a moment, and then laughed, before tossing Cavaan onto the floor by Shrike's feet.

This, then, was Gorkrusha.

Gorkrusha roared, raising his right arm as he charged towards Shrike, his drill-fist buzzing angrily. Shrike stood his ground as the ork closed the gap, bracing himself to attempt to deflect the attack. If he could angle Gorkrusha's fist at the wall, there was a chance the drill would bury itself in the chalk, causing him to become wedged, even for a moment. That was all the time Shrike would need to slit the creature's throat.

The very sight of the beast pounding towards him was a test of Shrike's mettle, as he raised his chainsword, intending to use it to batter the mechanical arm out of the way. The confined space of the tunnel would work to his advantage, and he hoped to use Gorkrusha's bulk against him.

The ork jabbed forwards with his drill-fist, with a blow aimed directly at Shrike's head. He sidestepped, just as Kadus opened fire over his shoulder, spraying Gorkrusha with a hail of bolter fire that burst in his face, cracking his metal jaw-plate and causing him to veer to the left.

The move caught Shrike unprepared and his chainsword snagged the drill blade, which wrenched it from his hands, chewing the metal casing and sending it spinning down the passageway behind him.

Gorkrusha was not to be easily dissuaded and rounded on Shrike, his left fist catching the Space Marine in the abdomen and knocking him back off his feet. Shrike slammed into the tunnel floor, his head striking the ground first, sending pain lancing through his skull. He had no time to consider what damage may have been caused, however, as the drill-fist descended a second later. He lurched, just in time for the spinning blade to score a deep furrow across his back, wrenching his dead jump pack from its housing. Gorkrusha's momentum carried

him forwards and the blade struck the floor, churning up clouds of dusty chalk as the soft material gave
way to the hardened metal.

Shrike was on his feet before Gorkrusha had righted
himself, only to see Kadus leaping forwards, the hilt
of his chainsword clutched in both hands. With his
full weight behind the blow, he buried the blade to
the hilt in Gorkrusha's chest, shattering a rib with a
sickening crunch.

Gorkrusha roared in pain, sweeping low and hard
with his fist and slamming Kadus back against the
wall. Shrike heard war-plate crack beneath the force
of the blow, and Kadus sunk to the ground beside
Cavaan, still and silent.

Shrike had no idea whether either of his brothers
still lived, but he wasn't sure it mattered; the rumbling of the seismic weapon had now reached a
crescendo, and all around them, the cliff was beginning to tremble. They were all going to die here.

Gorkrusha braced himself against the tunnel walls
as the ground shook violently, loosing fist-sized hunks
of chalk from the ceiling. The tunnel filled with dust,
and the ork hacked on the stuff as he drew breath.

Shrike, his respirator filtering the particles, saw his
chance. He grabbed for his combat knife – Corus'
blade – and darted forwards. He leapt to his feet,
twisting and slashing, severing the armoured cables
that fed Gorkrusha's drill-fist with power.

The drill ground to a sudden halt, and Gorkrusha,
realising what was happening, kicked out, catching

Shrike in the knee with his boot. The piston of his exoskeleton fired, snapping the foot down hard, and Shrike's knee exploded, the joint shattered beneath the force of the blow. He toppled forwards, crying out, but not before he'd buried his blade in the creature's chest, dragging it down in a long, ragged line as he sunk to the floor.

Gorkrusha howled as his chest opened like a flower's petals, exposing rubbery flesh and muscle, blood gushing down the front of his legs.

The ground seemed to shift suddenly as the weapon fired again, and a hunk of the wall detached with a splintering groan, striking Gorkrusha hard and sending him sprawling to the tunnel floor. A large crack had appeared in the ceiling, too, and more hunks of chalk were raining down from above, pounding Shrike's armour. He tried to get to his feet but his leg was completely buckled.

Gorkrusha, too, was struggling to get to his feet, pinned beneath the shattered wall, unable to lift his bulk. With the ceiling now coming down on top of them – the rest of the cliff along with it – there was nowhere for him to displace the massive hunk of chalk to get free. He roared, trying to dig his way out, but all he succeeded in doing was hastening the collapse of the tunnel around him. He was going to be crushed along with them.

Digging his fingers into the ground, Shrike dragged himself over to the prone Kadus. 'Brother?' he said, his voice weak over the vox. 'Kadus?'

Kadus didn't stir, but Shrike could tell from the sound of his respirator that he was still breathing. Cavaan, too, was alive, although his injuries were severe – Gorkrusha had run him through with his drill-fist, before tossing him away like a used rag, and the wound in his chest bubbled and wheezed with every breath.

The ground rumbled beneath them, and Shrike felt as much as heard the tunnel collapsing behind him, cutting off their path to the surface. The ork command had been destroyed, their weapon rendered useless.

He slumped back against the wall and closed his eyes. His fingers went to the bunch of corvia by his belt, and he cradled them in his fist.

It was done. He could be at peace now. All that awaited him was the forest.

With a splintering crack, the tunnel floor opened beneath him, and he fell into blackness.

Shrike woke to the burr of machinery. He couldn't feel his leg.

He realised he must have tumbled down into the workings of the seismic engine when the floor opened up, and lost consciousness from the fall. He was trapped in the darkness beneath the cliff, alone. He tried to sit up, but something was pinning him down; a chunk of the ceiling must have come down on top of him while he was out, effectively immobilising him. He laughed, and immediately wished he hadn't, as the gesture gave way to a thick, rasping cough. His lungs burned.

He'd expected to die in the tunnels, along with Kadus, Cavaan and the ork. Now, he was going to be forced to lie here, paralysed, until his armour eventually gave way and the weight of the collapsed ceiling crushed him, or else he bled out from his injuries. He sighed, resigned to his fate.

Something, however, wasn't right. He could feel cool air against the skin of his face. What had happened to his helm? Had it cracked in the fall? And if he could feel the air currents, did that mean there was a means of escape, a chance of reaching the outside world again?

He blinked, prising open his eyes. There was light here, too: lumens, but more than that – the watery fingers of dawn.

'Shrike?'

The voice seemed distant, but familiar. Groggily, he lifted his head.

He was lying on his back inside the hold of a Thunderhawk. His armour had been removed and he was strapped to a bench, his leg dressed in analgesic wrappings. The sound he had heard – what he had first taken to be the workings of the ork machine – was the sound of the engines groaning to life.

Kadus sat across from him, his helm removed, an expression of concern on his pale face. 'Kayvaan?'

'Aye, Kadus,' he said, surprised at the weakness of his own voice. 'So I see we both live to fight another day.'

'Cavaan, too,' said Kadus. 'His injuries are severe, but he'll survive this. As will you.'

Shrike laughed again. 'I do not understand how,' he said, 'But I am grateful for it.'

Kadus grinned. 'The orks were routed when the cliff came down. Shadow Captain Saak and the others searched the ruins for survivors.'

'Or to ensure Gorkrusha was dead,' said Shrike.

'Perhaps,' said Kadus. 'Regardless, I heard them over the vox. I'd managed to drag you and Cavaan halfway to the surface, and Saak took over, digging us the rest of the way out. You've been unconscious – you took a blow to the head when you fell into the workings of the machine. I'm afraid you're going to need a new helm.'

'I feel like I'm going to need a new everything,' said Shrike. 'Tell me, what of Gorkrusha? Did Saak verify his remains?'

A glimmer of something dark passed over Kadus' expression. 'Presumed buried beneath the cliff,' he said. Shrike could hear the uncertainty in his voice.

'You believe he survived,' said Shrike. It was a statement, not a question.

Kadus frowned. 'If *we* survived...'

Shrike turned away, staring out of the viewing slit as the Thunderhawk lifted into the waking sky. Had it all been for nothing? Surely not. Shrike simply couldn't believe that all of their sacrifices – Corus, Aarvus, Gradus, Hirus, Arkus, Ayros, Kadryn – had been for nought. They'd stopped the machine. He'd seen Gorkrusha go down, too. He'd gravely wounded him, scoring his chest open with a horrific gash. He'd seen the wall collapse upon him, seen him trying – and failing – to dig his way free.

Yet there was a part of him that knew Kadus was right. He hadn't seen Gorkrusha die. That meant there was a chance he, too, had made it out alive.

The Thunderhawk banked. From up here, the ruins of Shenkar Prime were like an ungainly patch of scar tissue across the surface of the world, criss-crossed by the massive, interlaced channels blasted into it by the ork weapon.

It still troubled Shrike that he had no sense of what the orks were doing. It seemed enough for the others to know that they were wreaking destruction upon this blighted world, but Gorkrusha was too clever for that. Shrike was sure of it. There had to be a reason why he would go to such lengths, to build his terrible machine, when his forces had already decimated the human cities and taken all that they wanted.

He glanced out of the viewing slit as the ship veered away into the cloud cover, and saw it for the first time – saw what Gorkrusha had really been doing on Shenkar.

The seismic agitator had been working to a strict design. Every crevasse or canyon Gorkrusha had opened in the surface combined to form a single glyph, smashed into the side of the world on a scale that was only visible from orbit. A grinning, animal-istic face.

That's what Gorkrusha had been doing here on Shenkar; that's what all of this was about. Territorial marking on a planetary scale.

It was grotesque. The loss of life involved was on an unimaginable scale. All for the gratification of a single greenskin.

Shrike turned back to Kadus, who was secured into a flight harness, watching him from across the hold. 'If he did survive, Kadus, we shall end him. No matter how long it takes, Gorkrusha will pay for what he did here – for the deaths of our brothers. In Corus' name, I shall hunt him down and put a round through his skull.'

Kadus said nothing, but the set of his jaw and the distant look in his eyes told Shrike everything he needed to know.

The Thunderhawk shuddered as it breached the atmosphere, and Shrike closed his eyes. The analgesics were causing him to feel drowsy. Now was the time to heal. Revenge would wait.

PART TWO

SHADOW CAPTAIN

Two birds perched upon the fallen branch, their heads bobbing and twitching like old maids, deep in conversation. Shrike wondered what they would say to one another if they really could speak. Would one warn the other of the warriors in the forest, the pale figures who bottled their spirits and carried their skulls into war? Would they even believe it?

Shrike could hardly believe it himself. Nor could he believe his luck. Barely half an hour had passed since the previous raven had taken wing, and now another two had arrived. Fortune was smiling upon him.

He observed them for a few moments, making his choice. The bird on the left kept rustling its wing in an awkward, ungainly gesture, as if the limb would no longer fold back into the correct position. He wondered if perhaps another of the initiates had attempted to grab it, and had injured the creature before it managed to get away. It would make for an easier target: slower, less likely to escape his grasp. It would be enough to see him through his initiation.

The other raven, however, was a much finer beast. Its feathers were slick and midnight-black, and there was something fierce and pure about it, something ethereal. He couldn't explain it, but he felt an odd sense of kinship with the bird, as if it were choosing him, as much as he was choosing it.

This, he knew, was his true test – did he take the easiest path, the quickest route to success, or did he take the path that *felt* right? Throughout all of the trials, Shrike had trusted his instincts. He was not yet a trained warrior, yet he had won through on passion, dedication and a deep belief in what was right. This was the true purpose of the trial, he realised: to reach an understanding of the spiritual, as well as the physical. This was a test of his nature as much as his stealth.

Perhaps this was where he had gone wrong the first time. He'd been in such a hurry to prove himself that he hadn't stopped to consider whether it felt right.

Shrike took a step out from behind the bough of the bolas tree. The other raven, the one with the damaged wing, must have seen or heard him, as it immediately launched itself from the branch, squawking loudly as it fluttered off into the forest.

The other raven turned its head, its beady eyes blinking as it regarded him. Shrike froze, suddenly unsure. Had he done the wrong thing? Was this bird, too, about to take wing in fear?

He fought the rising sense of panic. No. He was sure of this path. He knew, with a certainty he would stake his life upon, that he was doing what he was *meant* to do.

Shrike closed his eyes. He drew a thin, cool breath, dragging it down into his lungs. He moved his hands around so that they met before him, and he formed a cup, just as he had before, his fingers splayed to form a cage for the bird.

Keeping his eyes closed, he took another step towards the fallen branch. Still there was no sound of movement from the bird, no squawk of alarm. He allowed his senses to guide him, inching forwards, breathing steadily, slowing the frantic beating of his heart. He felt calm, for the first time in hours. He felt ready.

And then he moved. Shrike's hands shot out like lightning drawn to a wavering rod. His fingers closed around something soft and downy, and, almost afraid to open his eyes, to test that it was real, he peered down to see the raven there, cupped in his hands.

The bird did not protest. Not once did it fight for freedom, nor peck at him in fear. It simply sat there in his hands, calmly accepting of its fate.

Shrike raised his hands up, bringing the bird level with his face. He peered into its glossy eyes, searching for hidden secrets. But the bird would not reveal them today.

'Thank you,' he whispered, before reaching down and gently twisting its neck. Its body sighed once, and then went limp in his hands. 'Thank you.'

For a moment Shrike stood, cradling the dead bird in his hands. He felt overcome, ecstatic, even – not from the act of killing, which in itself was not a thing that he relished – but with the burning anticipation of everything this moment would precede. Pride, he knew, was a dangerous emotion, but he nevertheless allowed himself a small glimmer of satisfaction. He had proved himself worthy. The evidence of it was here, in his hands. He would claim his place amongst the hallowed ranks of the Raven Guard, and he would vow to uphold their sacred mission: to serve the Emperor of Mankind and protect those domains upon which the light of His Astronomican fell.

Handling the dead raven with a reverence his fellow clansmen would reserve for their deceased elders, he felt for the small leather purse that hung from his loincloth, and gently slipped the body inside. He tightened the drawstring and secured the purse in place. Now all he had to do was quit the forest and return to the village, where the imposing figure of Cordae would be waiting.

Cordae had overseen all of their trials. He, Shrike understood, was a keeper of the spiritual secrets of the Chapter – the one who judged, who weighed the souls of his brothers and deemed them worthy or unworthy. So, too, did he judge the initiates, and

Shrike had a sense that he could understand more than he could see with his eyes alone.

Unlike his brothers, who carried their corvia in small bundles from their belts, Cordae had adorned his armour with fetishes fashioned from the bones of a great Kiavahran roc, the giant, mountain-dwelling cousins of the raven Shrike had hunted in the forest. He wore its skull like a mask, atop the faceplate of his black helm, while its ribs formed a grisly brace across his chest. To many of the initiates he was a terrifying figure, a shamanic creature conjured from the very depths of space, come here to test them. To Shrike he was fascinating, a manifestation of all that the Raven Guard held dear, at one with the spirit of his chosen beast. Shrike patted the purse by his side. He only hoped that one day he could achieve a similar end.

He heard voices, and, surprised, turned to see Kadus and Corus rustling through the undergrowth, heading in his direction. Kadus, too, had stripped down to his loincloth and carried a limp bundle of feathers in his left hand. He was grinning broadly. Shrike felt a momentary surge of joy. Together, they could continue their journey into true maturity, just as they had since childhood. They had always talked of serving under the stars together, of joining the ranks of the Adeptus Astartes. Now that dream was to be realised.

Corus, on the other hand, appeared to be faring less well. He was still dressed in his tunic and skirts, now spattered with mud, and he seemed utterly dejected. In fact, as they approached Shrike, he could see that Corus was trembling – not in agitation, but in fear. Shrike supposed he was terrified of being left behind, of seeing Kadus and Shrike go off without him. Shrike could understand that. What he couldn't understand was why Corus was here, now, instead of out amongst the trees, hunting for his prey. Dusk would settle soon, like a blanket falling across the forest, and the trial would be over.

'How fare you, Kayvaan?' said Kadus, holding out his hand to present his winnings to Shrike.

Shrike grinned. 'I fear my bird is an even healthier specimen than yours, Kadus,' he said, patting his purse. 'While that mangy thing might just scrape you through.' Their eyes met, and they both burst out into excited laughter.

'Good news, indeed,' said Kadus. 'I would expect nothing less.'

Shrike grabbed his friend and placed a hand upon his shoulder. 'We have done it. Together, we have *done* it.' He looked to Corus, who was standing to one side, pretending to study the fallen branch from which Shrike had plucked his kill. 'And what of you, Corus? How fares your hunt?'

Corus turned, indicating the muddy stain upon his tunic. 'I fear I now have a better knowledge of the ditches in this miserable forest than I should ever wish to.'

'Ah,' said Shrike. He left Kadus' side, crossing to stand before Corus. 'Then surely you should be out *there,* Corus, and not here, with us. There is still time. You cannot give up, not now. The stakes are too high. I know you have it in you.'

Corus offered him a wan smile. 'Do I? I'm no longer so sure.'

'*I* am,' said Shrike. 'And so, too, is Kadus.'

'Indeed,' said Kadus, lending support. 'We cannot leave for Deliverance without you, Corus. It wouldn't be the same.'

'Then stay here with me, brothers, in the forest, while I find my own way in this hunt.'

Shrike looked to Kadus, who gave an almost imperceptible shrug. What harm could it do? He and Kadus had already secured their futures. Provided they made it back to the village before nightfall, they would be en route to Deliverance by morning, alongside those scarce few others who had proved themselves in the hunt. To stay and lend Corus their support seemed a small gesture. Kadus was right – to leave Corus behind would seem wrong, after all these many years together.

'Very well,' said Shrike. 'Here, I suggest you find a position behind this bolus tree. Soon enough, a raven may perch on this fallen branch. Kadus and I will wait over there.' He indicated a small patch of bushes where the two of them could easily conceal themselves.

Corus smiled. 'My thanks to you both. With your support, how could I possibly fail?' Shrike watched as Corus stepped behind the bolus tree, folding into the boughs, a silent, watchful sentinel.

With a last glance at Kadus, Shrike trekked over to the bushes and sank down into the loam to wait.

It had been decades since the Third Company had returned to Deliverance, and even longer since Shrike had found time to make the pilgrimage out here, to Kiavahr, to the forest of his youth.

It was just as he remembered it – peaceful, lush and bristling with life. He'd removed his helm, and for a moment he stood, breathing deeply, enjoying the damp, wild scent of the place that had once served as home. His time here was a distant memory, almost lost to the fog of age and war. He had been away for so long, been someone else for even longer.

Yet he retained a bond with the place, as all of his brothers did. Kiavahr was the womb that had given birth to him, the proving ground where he had become an initiate. Now he was a shadow captain, master of the Third Company of the Raven Guard. Yet it was here that he took his vow, here that he first learned what it meant to be a Space Marine, to pledge himself to a cause greater than himself.

It was here, too, that he had made his greatest mistake.

Shrike cradled the single, bleached skull in his fist. This was Corus' corvia, carried with him all the way from Shenkar. It had been years – long, difficult years – since Corus had been lost, and yet Shrike had honoured his promise, keeping the tiny raven skull safe, carrying it alongside his own. It had been a constant presence, a reminder of what had been lost, and it had sailed with him across the distant void, marched with him into battle on worlds of whispering ice, across harsh deserts populated by blood-worshipping traitors, and through minefields left behind by retreating greenskins.

Today, he had come to return it, to place it in the soil on Kiavahr and honour his lost brother. Many of the company had done the same; this was the duty of the Raven Guard, a pledge they took to one another to honour the spirits of the fallen.

Shrike had thought to bury the totem at the ritual site, half a mile from here – to place it alongside the thousands of others in the Fields of the Honoured Dead. Yet upon arrival, he'd had a better idea, and now he was winding his way through the forest, searching for a familiar tree.

He found it after only a short while, as if it were somehow calling to him, urging him on, deeper into the woods. The tree had grown in the intervening years, its roots now thick and muscular, writhing slowly across the forest floor. He stepped over them cautiously, aware that if he agitated them they might entangle him here and drag him beneath the trunk into one of its digestion sacs. He'd seen it happen as a child, when one of the hunters, grown too sure of himself, had try to wrest a captured debreek from one of the trees, thinking to take it for himself. The tree had gladly obliged, setting the debreek free, but taking the human for its meal instead.

Shrike glanced around the forest floor. It was too much to hope that the fallen branch from which he'd plucked his own corvia still remained; it had likely disintegrated in the meantime, returning to the earth in the same way that they all, inevitably must.

He estimated the spot where it had been, and crossed to it, dropping to his haunches. He used the tips of his fingers to dig a small hollow in the damp earth, clearing away handfuls of slippery leaves. *This* was where Corus' totem would rest.

Shrike held the bird skull over the hole, and thought of Corus. There had been mistakes, of course – on Shenkar, and before that. Costly mistakes.

Corus, however, had been a bold and unflinching warrior. He had led his brothers to victory on the killing fields of Asduk, fought the eldar to a standstill at Creve'tock, and pulled Shrike from the snapping jaws of a tyranid beast on Beluvious V. Yet Shrike had never forgotten what had happened here, in this forest, and to this day harboured a deep sense of responsibility for Corus' death. He had taken on that responsibility as a youth, that day in the forest, and as he'd watched his friend rise through the ranks of the Raven Guard, he had hidden that sharp feeling of disquiet, choosing not to speak of it, not even to Kadus. In doing so, he had compounded his error.

Did it matter? It was a question he had asked himself many times. Corus was gone, now, and perhaps it was only Shrike's conscience that remained to be salved. Yet he felt there was still something to be done, some gesture that would better honour his fallen brother. Shrike had to know that Corus had not died in vain.

'Shadow captain?'

He looked around to see Kadus standing on the edge of the glade. He, too, had removed his helm, and Shrike could see the sadness in his eyes. Kadus had been there, and had always known the truth. Returning here was as difficult for him as it was for Shrike.

'Yes, Kadus?'

'I regret to disturb you, particularly at this most delicate of moments, but there is urgent news.'

Shrike sighed. Such was his duty, even here, in the forests of Kiavahr. 'Go ahead.'

'The moon of Evenfall has succumbed to a series of devastating xenos attacks. The planet is already considered lost. The Imperial Navy is requesting assistance in arranging the evacuation of key assets.'

Shrike considered this for a moment. 'Evenfall... That's a little close for comfort. What of the Astra Militarum? Can they not provide the necessary forces?'

'The Astra Militarum have already deployed to the surface, shadow captain, along with support from the Adeptus Mechanicus. They've been unable to wrest control back from the xenos.'

'You're holding something back, Kadus. What is it you're not telling me?'

Kadus looked thoughtful. 'If you'll forgive me,

shadow captain,' he said, 'I think you should attend the briefing. There's something you should see.'

Shrike had no time for riddles, but something in the set of Kadus' jaw, the expression in his eyes, caused him to nod in acquiescence. He stood, closed his fist and quit the clearing.

Behind him, a raven landed in the small, empty hollow, pecked forlornly at the earth in search of grubs, and then took wing again, darting off into the forest.

The briefing took place inside a small bunker close to the training compound.

This was where the initiates were trained, amongst the shadow-fields of the complex, the nightmarish maze of moss-lined tunnels and warrens, the open plazas they were forced to cross unseen. This was where the Raven Guard became masters of stealth, traversing deadly traps and facing live gun emplacements as they ran, blindfolded, through staging points, learning to trust their instincts and pass in silence – judged all the while by the Chaplains who watched from these very bunkers, deciding which of them might live to become Space Marines.

Through the viewing port, Shrike could see the latest batch of initiates undergoing their rigorous physical trials in the courtyard, and turned away, squashing another surge of unwanted memories. He had to remain focused. There would be time to remember the past later.

A Thunderhawk had arrived from Deliverance just a short while earlier, bearing the news from Evenfall, along with a series of picts and vid-captures. When Shrike and Kadus had entered the room, they had found Phaeros, Arimdae, Kaask and Cavaan waiting for them. Kaask was outlining the present situation on Evenfall.

'As you're aware, shadow captain, Evenfall is a strategic asset. There's a cluster of research stations on the moon, along with a vast Ecclesiarchy outpost that covers approximately a quarter of the entire surface.'

'And the outpost wasn't adequately defended? What of the Sisterhood?' said Shrike.

Kaask frowned. 'As we understand it, the Sisterhood have so far managed to defend the walls, keeping the xenos at bay. Even supported by the Astra Militarum, however, the outpost is expected to fall within the next few days. The sheer quantity of greenskins means they're simply outnumbered.'

'Greenskins?' said Shrike, his interest piqued. 'In this sector?'

'That's what I wanted you to see,' said Kadus.

He reached for a dataslate, but Kaask stayed his hand. 'Before you do, shadow captain, it is important that you understand precisely what is at stake here. Evenfall is a planet shrouded in darkness, cast eternally in the shadow of its twin. The settlements are maintained by means of a series of lumen arcs – vast structures that span the sky, flooding the inhabited areas of the moon in artificial sunlight. These structures have been destroyed. Evenfall is a world in the midst of an eternal night.'

'All but one of them,' said Kadus.

'Indeed,' said Kaask. 'The moon has already been declared lost. The situation is now deemed irreparable. The engineering work to repair the lumen arcs would take centuries, and there are simply too many orks. If we lend our support, it will not be to save the planet, but to safeguard the evacuation of the key personnel and assets from the research stations and outposts.'

'I see,' said Shrike. He could sense they were still holding something back from him, evidently wary of his response. 'Now show me the damn picts.' He held his hand out for the dataslate.

Kaask stepped back, and Kadus passed Shrike the dataslate.

He studied the first pict for a moment. The arc of the small moon was nearly lost against the endless vista of the void. Any light that shone upon the surface of that world was lost from this perspective, taken from high in orbit – any light but one.

One of the lumen arcs had been transformed. The effort to effect such a change must have been tremendous – the very structure of the thing had been altered, reshaped, forced as if by will into a familiar shape, and left to burn, bright and vivid, like a scar upon the surface of the world.

It was a glyph Shrike had seen before, that he still

saw in his waking dreams: Gorkrusha's grinning, hateful face, staring up at him, taunting him.

'He's there. Gorkrusha is on that moon,' said Shrike.

Kadus nodded. 'He must have survived our encounter on Shenkar.'

'Now, after all these years,' said Shrike, 'he shows his hand.' To Shrike, it seemed like a sign, a gift. This was why he could not rest, why he'd been unable to strike all thoughts of Corus from his mind. While Gorkrusha still lived, Corus could not be at peace. His sacrifice on Shenkar amounted to nothing.

'The Imperial Navy need our support, shadow captain,' said Phaeros. 'I, too, was on Shenkar. I remember. Yet I feel I must counsel, now is not the time for vengeance. Now is the time to lend our strength to the evacuation.'

Shrike nodded. He looked to Cavaan. 'And you? What counsel would you offer this day, Cavaan?'

Cavaan looked from Kaask, to Kadus, to Shrike. When he spoke, his voice was tinged with a metallic rasp – the result of the injuries he had sustained on Shenkar, and the work that had to be carried out to repair him. He had come close to being entombed within a suit of Dreadnought armour, but had survived his initial surgeries well enough that such extreme measures had not been needed. He was still an outstanding warrior, and a valuable member of Shrike's company. 'There is wisdom in these warnings, shadow captain. I saw the destruction Gorkrusha wrought. First hand, I witnessed what he is capable of.' He paused, allowing his words to sink in. 'Now he has taken another world. If he is allowed to survive this conflict, what more will he do? How many worlds must fall before the beast is put down?'

Shrike nodded grimly. 'I see there is wisdom in both paths,' he said, 'and that we may yet find a means to accomplish both. The evacuation must proceed, and we must commit our forces to assisting the Navy and the Guard. Let us send word to that effect and make plans to deploy forthwith.'

'Yet you still mean to go after Gorkrusha?' said Arimdae. It was the first time he had spoken since Shrike had entered the room.

'I do,' said Shrike.

'I mean only to say, shadow captain, that if that is your will, then you have my support.'

Shrike nodded in acknowledgement. 'We leave within the hour for Deliverance. There we will mobilise the rest of the company, and the orks shall learn our wrath.' He turned and left the bunker, still clutching the dataslate.

Evenfall.

Shrike stared at the moon from the viewing slit of his Thunderhawk. What was it that had attracted Gorkrusha here, to this small moon on the outer rim of the Hadros system? More than just the gaudy lights, he was sure. Had he come looking for Shrike? Had he, too, been longing for vengeance, wishing to visit his wrath upon those who had beaten him on Shenkar?

It was possible. If it were true, though, didn't that mean that Shrike was leading his brothers into a trap, just as Corus and Saak had done so before him? Was history repeating itself?

From the surface below, the grinning visage of the ork stared up at him, mocking him, challenging him.

He sighed. Perhaps Kaask was right. Perhaps he was allowing the situation to needle him. One thing was clear – there were assets on that moon that the Imperium needed, for whatever reasons, and Shrike was not about to allow them to fall into enemy hands. The Raven Guard would assist with the evacuation. That was his primary duty.

Nevertheless, Gorkrusha awaited him, and he would see to it that the beast was put down, once and for all.

He turned away from the viewing slit as the ship began its descent, spiralling down through the thin atmosphere of the moon to avoid enemy fire from below. The vessel shook violently, heat shields blazing, as it swept through the cloud layer and burst out into the crisp, eternal night.

The pilot gunned the engines and the Thunderhawk skimmed low, banking to avoid a lazily climbing enemy rocket. It shot past their left wingtip and off into the distance, finally detonating in a colourful display, high up amongst the clouds.

They landed on a Skyshield landing pad, close to the heart of the Ecclesiarchy outpost. The Astra Militarum had co-opted the place as a base of operations, and it was from here, Shrike had been told, that their commanding officers were overseeing the evacuation efforts.

The fortress was impressive, with soaring, fortified bastions, like monoliths raised to the glory of war, and martyr's walls punctuated by vengeance batteries and firestorm redoubts. The heavy guns barked at the sky, causing the ground to tremble, and detonating crude ork gunships with every burst. Still, Shrike knew, it was too little, too late. The planet was already lost.

Shrike disembarked quickly, feeling somewhat confined and ill at ease within the hold of the Thunderhawk. He stepped down onto the landing pad and glanced up at the towering edifice before him. It was so tall that it seemed to scrape the very sky itself, a monument raised to the glory of the Emperor and dripping with all of the baroque glory that he had come to expect from the Ecclesiarchy. Gargoyles strained at their stone perches, anxious to protect the sanctity of the structure from these newcomers, while floating plinths drifted around the entrance, each ablaze with a brace of white candles.

'What of the others?' asked Shrike, without looking back. He could hear the footsteps of his command squad falling in behind him.

'Setting down in the regolith behind the Aegis defence lines, shadow captain,' said Phaeros from over his shoulder. 'They should be ready to deploy within the hour.'

'Tell them to make it quicker,' he said, heading for the entrance. 'This isn't going to take long.'

Shrike nodded to the two human guards who were standing in the mouth of the bastion. They both paled at the imposing sight of him – a captain of the Raven Guard, dressed in the beaked ebon armour of his Chapter. It was within his power to crush their skulls with a flick of his wrist, but he knew these to be good men, men who stood for the Emperor, who would give their lives to see justice done and the ways of the Imperium upheld.

Inside, the lobby was just as grand as the building's exterior. He could see the stars overhead, projected onto the vaulted ceiling by an enormous camera obscura, pointed to the heavens. Terra's sun, he suspected, was the tiny, glowing dot at the heart of the projection, picked out in filigreed gold; a reminder of the cradle of the Imperium, the womb from which humankind was born. Shrike had never walked its hallowed halls, but he'd heard tales of the days of Corax and his parleys with the Emperor Himself. The place reminded him of the temple he had seen on Shenkar, all those years ago: holy, haunted and melancholy.

'Shadow Captain Shrike?'

Shrike looked down to see a human in a black uniform standing nervously by his elbow. 'I am he,' said Shrike. His voice echoed in the vast chamber, lending its deep baritone an even more imposing weight.

'General Hultriss is awaiting you, sir,' said the human. 'If you'd like to come this way.'

Shrike had little time for these strategic debates – he knew what needed to be done and was anxious to get on with it. Nevertheless, he needed the data the humans had so far managed to collate, as well as to ensure that their plan was robust.

He followed the aide along a narrow passage-way – at least, narrow by the standards of a Space Marine – and into a large, open room that might once have been a mess hall, but was now a bustling oper-ations room. Pict screens and hololithic displays had been mounted at regular intervals upon long trestle tables, and topographical maps of the moon's sur-face had been plastered upon the walls. Reports were coming in from the front, and an army of menials, aides and servitors were busy manning the vox and altering the displays to provide real-time informa-tion on numerous battles.

Shrike ducked his head under the door and stepped inside. Immediately, two men were before him, offer-ing up salutes. 'Shadow Captain Shrike, you have my gratitude,' said a lean, middle-aged man in the green fatigues of the Astra Militarum. He wore a slew of medals upon his chest, and bore a lurid, purple scar, which stretched from his left ear down across his dark-skinned throat. 'I am General Hultriss of the Guard, and this is Admiral Sheol of the Navy. We're coordinating the evacuation.'

Shrike nodded. 'Well met,' he said. He was staring past them, at a vid-capture of a battle being played out on one of the screens. The Astra Militarum were being massacred, cut down in swathes by greenskins riding out of the night on speeding buggies, hosing them down with explosive rounds. He reached up and unclasped his helmet, mag-locking it to his leg. He looked the admiral up and down – a stiff looking man in a blue uniform with golden braids. He was tall for a human, and wiry, and much of his face was hidden behind a thick, brown beard. He eyed Shrike nervously, as if hanging on the Space Marine's next words.

'How may we be of assistance, general?' he said, addressing Hultriss. 'I understand your forces are struggling to keep the xenos at bay?'

'Well, you can see for yourself,' said Hultriss, waving at the screen. 'We've lost thousands of men. We're outgunned and outnumbered, and it's all we can do to keep them busy. While they're slaughtering their way through our platoons, we're ferrying all of the assets out of the back door.' He glanced at Sheol.

'We have two frigates in orbit,' said Sheol. 'The orks don't appear to be concerned with them, preferring to slaughter whatever is closest at any given time. A flotilla of smaller vessels is ferrying the evacuees up to orbit, but at the rate we're losing men, the orks are going to push through our defences before the job is done.'

'Then the Raven Guard will assist you in the field,' said Shrike.

'My thanks,' said Hultriss. 'Give us as much time

as you can. Then we pull out and abandon this Emperor-forsaken place to the orks.'

'There is one other thing,' said Shrike. 'The ork warlord responsible...?'

'Gorkrusha,' said Sheol. 'I presume you saw the lumen arc as you came in?'

'Indeed,' said Shrike. 'I've had dealings with the creature before. Tell me, what intelligence do you have regarding his location?'

'We believe he's making preparations to flee, leaving his filthy kin to run riot while he hunts down another planet to destroy.'

'His present location?' pressed Shrike.

Hultriss crossed to one of the maps on the wall. It was an aerial shot of the battlefield, captured from orbit. The image was pixelated, but just about discernible. Hultriss drummed his fingers on it. Shrike noticed one of them was missing. 'He was last seen in the vicinity of this power station,' he said. 'It's the unit that supplies the lumen arc he's using to broadcast his face into space. We had an idea to blow it up, preferably with him inside.'

'But your men never returned?' ventured Shrike.

Hultriss nodded. 'I despatched a detachment of storm troopers. Some of the best men we had. They didn't even get close. Gorkrusha's not taking any chances. He's got some sort of titanic war machine out there. They never stood a chance.'

Sheol was frowning. 'You're not thinking of going after him, are you, shadow captain?'

'Do not fear, admiral. Your men will have all the support they need. The evacuation will be completed.'

'And you'll be on the ground with your troops?'

'Something like that,' said Shrike. He turned to the door. 'We deploy in twenty minutes.' He stalked out of the room, his boots clanging on the marble floor as he went.

Shrike watched as the final Raptor Wing battalion rumbled overhead, Stormtalons weaving through the monumental spires of the Ecclesiarchy outpost. Their engines churned at the thin air, weapons humming as they powered to full capacity. Below them, Landspeeders skimmed across the battlefield, while bike squadrons churned up the soft earth and Bladewing formations darted around their flanks, their jump packs roaring.

The Raven Guard were not here to win a war. Even the full might of the Third Company would be as nothing when pitched against an enemy so numerous and entrenched. Instead, they would harry them from above and below, striking fast and deep at the largest concentration of orks, moving on to their next target before the xenos had time to understand what had hit them. It was a tactic that had served them well on numerous occasions, and would keep the greenskins busy while Hultriss and Sheol saw to the evacuation.

The last of the Stormtalons disappeared over the rooftops, even the glowing trails of their engines soon enveloped by the cloak of night. The all-pervading darkness here on Evenfall was an advantage to those so schooled in stealth; Shrike's assault squads would circle the enemy, close in, and shred them apart with their lightning claws, before melting away into the shadows once again. Shrike could almost anticipate the confusion of the orks, and he relished it.

He turned to Arimdae. 'Assemble the Shadow Force. We go to war.'

'For Gorkrusha?'

'Aye. For Gorkrusha.'

'Do you think me foolhardy, Kadus?' said Shrike, as the two of them soared above the muddy fields of war on plumes of flame. Shrike's lightning talons crackled and popped in the wind, charged and expectant.

'I think that you're the shadow captain,' said Kadus, 'and that I trust you now as I have always trusted you.'

'That's not what I asked,' said Shrike. 'You should have been a politician, Kadus. You evade answers almost as well as you evade capture.'

Kadus laughed. 'For what it's worth, Kayvaan – I, too, long to see that beast dead. There is a debt to be paid, and we are the only two who know it.'

'Aye,' said Shrike. 'This may be our chance to make it right.'

'It would bring me much needed peace,' said Kadus. 'Although I fear our brothers do not understand. 'Phaeros, for instance, and even Cavaan, see nought but vengeance driving your actions here

today. They know not of Kiavahr, and Corus. They
see only blind and furious rage.'

'A beautiful rage,' said Shrike. 'A pure rage.'

'Perhaps so,' said Kadus, 'but is that what you wish
to teach them? Is this the best way for them to march
to war, instilled with righteousness and anger? Is that
our way? I fear it is not. I fear it breeds impetuous-
ness, when what is needed is cool decisiveness and
a keen mind.'

'You are wise, my friend,' said Shrike. 'Yet we are
on a path, and I dare not veer from it now. Gorkrusha awaits us.'

'Then you are once more the shadow captain, and
once more, I trust you until the end,' said Kadus.

'And you are once more the politician,' said Shrike.

Up ahead, the world was aglow. Here, the light
from the bastardised lumen arc scorched the earth,
withering the fauna and baking the land itself like a
nightmarish desert. They were deep behind enemy
lines, having left the fighting behind them almost a
mile earlier. It had been a simple matter to butcher
their way through the thick of the fighting, making
use of the confusion caused by the arrival of the
Stormtalons and the wicked burr of their guns, chewing up the enemy with every overhead pass.

Additionally, a Landspeeder was up ahead, skimming across the baked earth, spotting for any sign
of the enemy and reporting back. They'd already
managed to avoid two trains of ork buggies, ferrying
reinforcements to the front. Shrike had considered

disrupting them, but knew it would not make a material difference to the efforts taking place in the shadow of the Ecclesiarchy outpost, and that was all that mattered. That and Gorkrusha.

Cavaan's voice crackled over the vox. 'We have visual on the power station.' He paused. 'Captain... you might want to consider your options.'

It was almost impossible to disappear in this hideous, glaring light, but it caused the shadows of buildings to run long and deep, and so the rest of his Shadow Force scattered amongst the outbuildings that crowded the edges of Gorkrusha's encampment, here in this old industrial complex.

Shrike ran on ahead, keeping low, using what shelter he could find to remain out of view.

Presently, he located the Landspeeder. The crew had pulled it to a halt on a dusty ledge, overlooking a wide but shallow depression in the earth. He crept up beside it, acknowledging the others, and peered over the edge.

A large force of greenskins had gathered in the shadow of the power station, itself a simple complex, comprising a handful of squat buildings and a bank of pylons laid out in a neat grid. It had once been a human structure, but the orks had adapted it, bolting on strange assemblages.

The orks were festooned with banners in myriad vibrant colours – reds, yellows and blues – like a patchwork of children's drawings. These creatures, though, were not from the fanciful imaginings of children, but the blackest nightmares of men. There were hundreds of them, arranged in ragged bands, their armour spattered with the same primitive colours as their flags. Strange tanks – amalgams of scrap, buggies, bikes and flying machines – flanked the milling throng. Two enormous war machines, erected in the parody of an orkish form and similar to the machine he had seen on Shenkar all those years ago, sat squat at the back, still and lifeless.

Before them all, standing on a platform in the shadow of a vessel that might have once been an Imperial Valkyrie, was Gorkrusha. Shrike recognised him immediately – the mechanical arm with its deadly drill-fist; the exoskeleton, which now appeared to extend up to cover his entire torso; the winking red eye; the brace of tusks. This was the creature he had fought on Shenkar and seen buried alive. This was the beast he had thought slain, and who had miraculously survived.

Worse, Shrike saw that he had almost missed his chance. Hultriss had told him that the warlord was making preparations to leave Evenfall. He'd been right – the cannibalised Valkyrie was powering up its engines at that very moment, blowing sand and dust in a great storm behind it.

The ork war party had clearly gathered to celebrate his departure, before – Shrike assumed – returning to the fervour of the nearby battle.

He was going to miss his chance.

Cavaan and Arimdae had now circled the ridge and

come to join him by the Landspeeder, surveying the massed ork forces below.

'Gorkrusha walks away. *Again,*' said Cavaan, through gritted teeth.

'No,' said Shrike. 'I cannot allow that.'

'Shadow captain, an assault on his position now would certainly end in failure,' said Arimdae, his voice level and matter of fact. 'We are but twenty. This false dawn would not serve us well.'

'You're right,' said Shrike. He stood watching Gorkrusha as the ork paced back and forth on the platform, saluting his troops in celebration of his victory and firing rounds off into the sky. 'Yet there is a way. I might yet confront him, alone, on that platform, before he boards his transport off world.'

'Shadow captain,' said Cavaan, 'it's certain death.'

'Indeed,' said Shrike. 'For both of us.'

'Shadow captain, I would ur–' Shrike didn't hear the rest, as he fired up his jump pack and made a run for the lip of the depression.

He leapt into the air, angling his body like a thrown dart, the tips of the Raven's Claws pointed directly at the platform and its lone, gloating occupant.

Kadus saw what happened next from behind the cover of a foetid, stinking moisture farm, from where he'd been observing the proceedings on the platform with a growing sense of frustration. One minute Gorkrusha had been bellowing words of encouragement to his ecstatic crowd of onlookers, the next he'd turned his attention towards something roaring towards him out of the sky.

Kadus followed his gaze, half expecting to see the shadow of an Imperial Valkyrie or similar gunship, but his hearts leapt in both fear and amazement at the sight of a single figure, adorned in black-and-white power armour, streaking through the air towards the platform.

It took a moment for Kadus to register it was Shrike. The shadow captain's lightning claws were sparking, and his jump pack roared, leaving a bright scar across the sky as he sailed directly at the ork warlord.

He meant to assassinate the creature there, Kadus realised, in full view of his gathered troops, and to prevent him from ever leaving upon the transport ship. It seemed so mindless.

There was no time to act, no chance of altering what was about to occur. Kadus could only watch, breathless, as Shrike thundered into full view.

For a moment, Kadus believed that Shrike was going to succeed, that he would skewer the ork through his chest, rending him apart, flesh, bone and steel – but then Gorkrusha stepped to one side, raised his drill-fist and swept it before him in a wide, defensive arc.

It was a bold, dangerous move, but Gorkrusha's timing was perfect. The metal fist caught Shrike in the shoulder as he came down and, unable to slow his momentum, he went tumbling into an uncontrollable spiral. He crashed into the platform, splintering the plascrete with the force of his landing. His jump pack puttered to a stop, and Shrike moved, trying to right himself, trying to get back to his feet.

He was too slow, however, and the ork was upon him immediately. The hulking figure stooped over the shadow captain, sweeping him up in his massive fist. Gorkrusha held him there for a moment, dangling by the throat, and then, as if disposing of a trinket he no longer cared for, cast him into the spinning engine of the nearby Valkyrie.

The engine sputtered for a moment, before detonating with a loud crump. Flames guttered, bright and intense, and then the automatic safety systems cut in, and the fire was swiftly doused. The vehicle shook but the other engine was more than capable of compensating for the sudden loss.

There was no sign of Shrike. His body must have been chewed apart by the engine and then incinerated by the flames. There was no way anyone could have survived.

The whole thing had just been so... perfunctory. In the blink of an eye, Shrike was dead. No ceremony, no great battle.

Kadus had always assumed Shrike's death would be glorious – hard fought against a worthy foe, a life given, in the end, through noble sacrifice, to clinch victory for his brothers. An *honourable* death. Gorkrusha had stolen that from him. Worse, there was now no chance that Kadus could reclaim Shrike's corvia. His passing would go unmarked in the Fields of the Honoured Dead.

The ork turned to the gathered throng, and roared. Even from across the dust bowl, Kadus felt the bestial power of it, as a low rumble in his gut. The crowd cheered, firing their weapons indiscriminately into the sky, whooping and clamouring for their leader. Shrike had not simply failed – he had handed Gorkrusha another victory, this time in full view of his troops. Instead of deposing the creature, he had inadvertently strengthened his position.

Kadus stood, reaching for his bolt pistol. His brother was dead. He would mete out what vengeance he could before he, too, lost his life.

He felt a restraining hand on his arm. 'No, brother,' said Kaask. 'Consider your actions. That is not what he would want. It was a reckless thing the shadow captain did, but he did it alone. He knew it would not end well, whether he managed to destroy the beast or not. Do not waste your own life trying to avenge him. We better serve our duty by returning to the outpost and aiding the evacuation. You must take charge now.'

Cavaan and Arimdae were calling to him over the vox, their voices urgent, desperate to move in on the ork warlord in their captain's wake. Kaask was right – if he didn't take charge, if he didn't issue orders now, the Shadow Force would lose cohesion.

Kadus gritted his teeth as he watched Gorkrusha embark into the Valkyrie – marked, of course, with his own grinning visage. The door slid shut, and the vessel rose slowly away from the platform, banked and shot up into the sky, its damaged engine leaving a thick trail of inky smoke behind it.

Kadus turned to Kaask. 'Assemble the others. We retreat to the outpost and do what we can to hasten the evacuation. We focus on our primary mission. The sooner we're off this damn ruin of a world, the better.'

In the distance, the ork rabble gave a final cheer, and began to disassemble, making ready for war.

'Dead?' said Hultriss. Even over the hololith, the incredulity was written all over his face.

Kadus, along with Kaask and Phaeros, was standing by the Landspeeder, peering at the hololith projector as he delivered the fateful news to the commander of the Guard.

'He should never have gone after Gorkrusha,' said Sheol, shimmering into view. 'I knew that it would end like this. That creature is unbeatable.'

'No,' said Kadus. 'You will show some respect. You have no right to question the decision of a shadow captain of the Raven Guard.' He glowered at the admiral, who paled at the sudden ferocity of Kadus' rebuttal. 'And understand this – no creature is unbeatable. Particularly a filthy greenskin such as Gorkrusha. Shrike understood that. He knew the power of leadership. He gave his life in an attempt to unseat the commander of the ork forces, knowing full well what impact such an action could have upon the morale of his forces. Look at you, for example. How you cower at the mere mention of his name. There is power in that. Shrike sought to undermine it, to make all of our work here easier.'

The admiral fell silent. The moment stretched.

'What now?' said Hultriss.

'Now we return to assist our brothers in defending the evacuation,' said Kadus. 'Expect our arrival at the bastion shortly.' He cut the link, and the hololith shimmered and blinked out.

'What you say may be true, brother, but Shadow Captain Shrike also sought to conclude a very personal vendetta,' said Kaask. 'Understand I do not question his judgement in this matter.'

Kadus bunched his fist as he confronted Kaask. 'Do not question his judgement? You've done nothing but!'

'It was my duty to challenge the shadow captain, just as it was yours. I never sought to undermine him,' said Kaask.

'Nor does it matter,' said Phaeros. 'Not when there is work still to be done.'

'Aye,' said Kadus. 'There is that. There is ork blood to be shed. Come, let us rejoin our brothers in battle and honour our dead with the blood of our enemies.'

'Tell me, general – how proceeds the evacuation?' said Kadus.

They had been forced to fight their way to the

outpost, carving a bloody swathe through the ranks of feral greenskins. The battlefield was ablaze, Stormtalons razing the ork ranks with autocannons, while bike squads ripped through their midst, rending and slashing as they passed. Even the hardened warriors of the Adepta Sororitas had now abandoned their watch-towers and spilled out into the field, Rhinos churning the dusty regolith, their bolters chattering, mowing down each wave of greenskins as it came. Nevertheless, the tide of battle was not turning in their favour. The orks were encroaching faster than anyone had predicted, and now Kadus brought news of orkish reinforcements, including their two enormous war machines, heading towards the outpost.

Now, Kadus, Phaeros and Kaask stood in the control room at the heart of the Imperial bastion, coordinating their next move.

'Two hours until the assets are secure.' Hultriss frowned. 'Although there'll be many, many more left on the surface.'

'Two hours, then,' said Phaeros, unmoved. 'The ork reinforcements will be here before then. We must strike fast and hard, prevent the reinforcements from joining the main assault.'

'Then you'll manage without me,' said Kadus. 'I will see to it that the shadow captain's mission is completed. Gorkrusha's heat signature will still be traceable. I'm taking one of the Thunderhawks and going after him.'

'You'll do no such thing.'

Kadus turned on the spot, furious at the temerity of this interruption.

In the doorway stood an imposing figure in battered black-and-white armour. He was streaked in soot and mud, his armour pitted, the beak of his helmet broken and twisted. A deep gouge in his chest-plate revealed a wound that was, even now, seeping dark blood. It spattered on the floor by his feet.

'*Shrike*?'

'Kadus,' said Shrike, by way of acknowledgement. He turned to Hultriss. 'General, I apologise for the mess, and for the interruption.'

'I... Well... I...' The human was utterly lost for words.

'How?' asked Kadus.

'I may have failed to kill the ork, but an engine is a far less hardy foe,' said Shrike.

For a moment, a stunned silence descended on the room, as each of them absorbed what had happened. They'd left him for dead, abandoned him behind enemy lines, in the midst of a thousand orks. And yet here he stood – battered, bruised, but alive.

Finally, Kadus spoke. 'Then together, we can still go after him. It's not too late.'

Shrike hung his head. 'It was always too late,' he said. 'I made a mistake, Kadus. The mission here was never about visiting our revenge on Gorkrusha. It was a fool's errand, and I was the fool. The moon was lost well before we arrived.'

'What now, then?' asked Phaeros.

'We do as you suggested, Phaeros. Leave the Astra Militarum to defend the walls, and hold back the ork reinforcements until the last of the transports have left the surface. The evacuation is our priority. Only... I believe there may yet be a way to rid the Imperium of this green scourge as we leave.' Shrike entered the room, crossing to the nearest map. 'The lumen arcs, general. How did Gorkrusha destroy them?'

'He damaged the regulators,' said Hultriss. 'Leaving no way to control their output. We were forced to cut the power before they went nova.'

'And if we turned them back on?'

'The entire surface of the moon would be seared. Nothing could survive. It would be like being thrown into the surface of a sun,' said Hultriss.

Shrike nodded. He looked to Kaask, soliciting his opinion. 'We weaponise the moon itself,' said Kaask. 'Finish the evacuation, and then burn what's left. There are hundreds of thousands of orks out there. When Gorkrusha's fleet comes to collect them, he'll find nothing but a smouldering cinder.'

'And what of the remaining civilians? Not to mention the last of the Guard?' This from Sheol, who was listening intently, arms folded across his chest. He was clearly not enamoured with Shrike's plan.

'We were never going to make it off this damnable planet alive,' said Hultriss. 'I knew that coming into it. You go, Sheol, and get those assets to where they're supposed to be. My men and I will keep the

orks busy until the bitter end. I can think of no better send off than that. Watching a new dawn rise on
a dead world, and seeing the enemies of the Imperium shrivel and die.'

'The words of a true soldier,' said Shrike. 'You are a
brave man, General Hultriss. The Raven Guard will
honour you.' He glanced pointedly at Sheol. 'Now,
tell me, how do we get that power back on? We do
not have much time.'

'There are three stations,' said Hultriss, 'just like the
one powering Gorkrusha's lumen arc.' He pointed
them out on the map. 'It's a chain. Power one, then
the next, then the third, and the grid comes online.
Once they're up and running, you'll have less than
an hour to get off-planet before the entire place is
burned to a crisp.'

'Not to mention, those stations will be swarming
with orks,' added Sheol.

'Leave that to us,' said Shrike. 'We strike hard and
fast. Minimal deployment. Combat squads and Tech-
marines only. We cannot forget that the evacuation
is our priority. There'll be three teams. I'll lead one,
Kadus takes another, Kaask the third. Phaeros, you
coordinate the consolidation here at the outpost, and
ensure we're ready to hand over to Hultriss' men
when the time comes to leave.'

'Three stations?' said Kadus.

'Time we laid some ghosts to rest,' said Shrike. 'This
isn't Shenkar. We've been in the darkness too long,
Kadus. All of us. It's time we stepped into the light.'

Kadus nodded. 'Then let us set this place ablaze, and give the orks something to remember us by.'

'Aye,' said Shrike. He glanced at Sheol. 'You know what you must do, admiral.'

'Indeed,' said Sheol.

'May the Emperor guide you, shadow captain,' said Hultriss, as Shrike started for the door.

'I believe that He always does,' said Shrike.

The power station was near enough an exact replica of the one Shrike had seen earlier, with a series of small buildings ranged alongside a neat grid of power coils, now adapted by the orks, bristling with additional data-spires and crude antenna. These were connected to a towering column that rose high into the starry ever-night, reaching beyond even the limit of Shrike's vision. This column, he presumed, stretched all the way up to the lumen arcs themselves, which scraped the thin atmosphere, criss-crossing the world like taught ribbons. Now, the arcs were dark and cold; soon they would burn with the light of the Emperor Himself, cleansing this blighted moon of its xenos oppressors.

The darkness here was near absolute, a thick, velvet cloak draped across the world, broken only by the occasional flash of an exploding incendiary device, or the distant glow of sky-bound engines. On the horizon, Navy ships ploughed through the night, riding on plumes of billowing smoke as they ferried their payloads to the waiting frigates. Closer, the battle continued to rage, generating a constant background hum. Shrike tuned it out.

Orks were picking over the remains of dead humans: the remnants of a Guard platoon, evidently slaughtered as they'd tried to reclaim the power station, probably some days ago. Their corpses were bloated and had long since succumbed to rigor mortis, twisting them into grotesque forms, monstrous caricatures of the people they had once been.

Shrike was in no mood for subtlety, however; time was against them, and he would *not* be late. Not this time.

The first didn't even have a chance to cry out as Shrike's Raven's Claws entered its chest, crackling and spitting, before rending it in half, leaving its remains slumped over the corpse of the Guardsman it had been looting. The second saw him coming and tried to run, but took only three steps before its upper half slid to the floor, suddenly separated from its legs. Shrike paid no heed to its moaning as he stormed on, heading for the largest of the three squat buildings. Behind him, the chatter of bolter fire told him that his veterans were seeing to another handful of errant orks.

Shrike reached the door behind Vaal, who turned his bolt pistol on the lock, blowing the mechanism. The door swung open, revealing a small chamber beyond, and an alarm blared from deep inside the substation.

Emergency lumens cast a pale glow over everything

inside, softening the harsh lines of the control stations. Once again, the orks had left their mark, daubing glyphs across consoles and wiring boxes of their crude xenos tech into the terminals.

An inner door, hanging open, led to another room beyond. It was from within this second room that the alarm was trilling.

Shrike entered the room, crossing to the control station. Vaal slipped in behind him, while the others took up position by the door, keeping guard.

Behind him, the Techmarine, Goral, lumbered into the room. He crossed to the control panel, mechadendrites whirring as he searched for the correct dial.

Shrike heard a snarl from the doorway into the other room, and sensed Vaal fall back, raising his bolt pistol. Shrike reached for his own weapon, drawing it and firing it in one fluid motion, never taking his eyes off the panel of levers and dials before him.

The ork in the doorway sighed almost peacefully, and slumped forwards, a hole through the centre of its forehead.

'Kadus? Kaask?' Shrike called over the vox. 'Are you in position?'

There was a hiss of static, and then Kaask's voice came onto the line. 'In position, shadow captain.'

'Then bring your station online,' said Shrike.

'Affirmative.'

A moment later, one of the needles on the control panel swung gently around, indicating the power level was rising.

'Kadus?' said Shrike. 'What is your position?'

He was met with only humming silence in return.

'Kadus?'

Shrike paused. Had Kadus run into trouble? Failure now would mean the entire enterprise was doomed – he didn't have time to despatch a second team to the other station and still make the evacuation before Phaeros ordered the Thunderhawks to take wing. More than that, he worried for Kadus' life. Had he allowed his fear of the past to interfere with the successful prosecution of his mission?

'Shadow captain?' said Goral.

The indicator dial on the control panel was now continuing its sweep around to the right as the power surged in the grid. 'Kadus?' Shrike said, again, knowing that only his brother could be behind this. 'Are you there?'

'Aye, shadow captain,' came Kadus' stuttering response. 'Met a little resistance here at the station, but I can confirm that the power level is now rising.'

'Confirmed,' said Shrike. 'Goral. Initiate the power.' The Techmarine turned the dial on the control panel, and the needle jumped as the energy was unleashed. With no regulators, the power would continue to build, overloading the lumen arcs until they detonated in a nova so powerful that it would be seen from Terra itself.

Light flooded the station as the power reached the arcs up above, pooling in through the open door. He stepped outside, retinal lenses compensating for the harsh glare. The moon looked like a different world in the baking daylight, and the extent of the orks' devastation became truly apparent. There was little left here worth saving, besides the many skulls of the dead.

Shrike checked the chronometer in his helm display. 'Rendezvous at the outpost as planned. Don't be late. This planet will be nothing but a burned cinder within the hour.'

He waited for Kaask and Kadus to confirm, and then gave the order to retreat. Within moments, the six ebon-armoured figures had disappeared into the false dawn.

From orbit, the moon glowed like a miniature sun, all trace of Gorkrusha's glyph lost amidst the blinding light of the detonating lumen arcs. Shrike knew that everything on the small planet was already dead, baked alive by the harsh radioactive glow that had seared flesh to bones and blasted bodies to ashen shadows like a nuclear storm.

'It was a brave sacrifice,' said Shrike. 'The man, Hultriss. He gave his life willingly to ensure the destruction of a million enemies of the Imperium.'

'Perhaps, in another time, he might have served alongside us, as a brother,' said Kadus.

The two of them were mag-locked in the hold of their Thunderhawk as it ploughed through the void, surrounded by the rest of their small fleet.

'I believe he might have been worthy,' said Shrike.

He peered out of the window at the corona of the burning moon. 'It is not yet over. There are other fallen worlds bearing his glyph, from which he might rebuild his armies.'

'Perhaps,' said Kadus. 'And yet, today was a victory, no matter how bitter. We dealt the orks a vicious blow. It will not go unnoticed.'

'Indeed,' said Shrike. 'Gorkrusha will know the name Kayvaan Shrike. Soon enough he will feel my claws.'

He watched through the viewing slit as Evenfall suddenly expanded outwards, trebling in size as the lumen arcs went nova, vaporising the surface of the moon and turning the once-dead core into molten slurry. Enormous jets of plasma boiled away into space, ejected from the roiling face of the new sun.

The Thunderhawk turned, falling in-line with the others, and set a course back to Deliverance, and home.

PART THREE

CHAPTER MASTER

The raven circled the fallen branch, rustling amongst the leaves. Shrike studied Corus, who was pressed against one of the boughs of the bolus tree. He hadn't moved in some time, and Shrike was now beginning to wonder if he'd even realised the bird was there. He'd shown no sign that he intended to move. He just continued to stand there, as if frozen to the spot.

The light was beginning to wane now, the long fingers of the afternoon reaching through the towering tree trunks, trying desperately to cling on before they were dragged once more into darkness. Soon, Shrike and Kadus would leave. The village was still a mile away, beyond the edge of the forest, and whatever happened here, he would not be late. He would place his raven on the dais before Cordae and claim his place amongst the other initiates. His loyalty to Corus was great, but it did not extend to failure.

The bird hopped up onto the dead branch. It twisted on the spot, and then lifted its head and cawed. The sound carried through the empty clearing, sharp and piercing, full of sadness and lament. It ruffled its damaged wing and seemed to look directly at Shrike, who still crouched behind a nearby bush beside Kadus.

Despite the bird's sudden call to arms, Corus still showed no sign of movement. Shrike was growing impatient with him. He *knew* what to do. They'd been practising together for months. The other trials had proved no obstacle to him. He'd demonstrated his physical and mental stamina beyond any doubt, along with his willingness to accept orders and his deep sense of loyalty and duty. Where many had fallen, exhausted and unable to continue, Corus had forged ahead, calling for Shrike and Kadus to follow. Cordae himself had singled him out, and the other hopefuls whispered amongst themselves that Corus had already been selected for greater things.

Now, though, he seemed frozen, unable to take the final, necessary step.

Shrike glanced at Kadus, but he was watching the bird through the gaps between the leaves. He wanted to stand and shake Corus by the shoulders, to wake him from whatever reverie was holding him back.

And then Corus suddenly jerked to life. He shot

out from behind the tree, darting towards the fallen branch, his hands cupped hungrily before him. Shrike knew immediately that he had moved too fast, too suddenly. The raven erupted in a blur of feathers, launching itself into the air to avoid his grasping, greedy hands.

It cawed again, setting other birds bursting to life in the canopy overhead.

In the memories that he would revisit so often in the future, what happened next was like a series of sudden, jarring stills, like picts captured and replayed in a slow, stuttering sequence.

The bird flew directly at Shrike. It was as if it knew he was there, as if it had been waiting for him to leap up from behind the bush. It came for his face, panic in its eyes, and veered only at the last moment, its wings spread wide as it tried to manoeuvre. Shrike turned his head, attempting to avert his eyes from its thrashing beak and claws, but his hand shot out, as if by its own volition, and the bird seemed to fly directly into his outstretched palm.

He closed his fist around the squawking, flapping bird, and felt it grow still, its heart thrumming, wild and scared. He looked down at it, its wing now hanging broken and limp, its beak silently hinging open in fear and pain. He tightened his grip and felt its life slip away.

For a moment, there was only silence in the glade. Then Kadus stood, staring at Shrike, his eyes full of wonder. He seemed lost for anything to say.

Corus ran over, his boots kicking up clods of sodden leaves. 'You did it, Kayvaan.'

Shrike relaxed his grip, still looking down at the dead bird in his palm. 'I did what?'

'You caught another raven. Now all three of us can claim victory in the hunt.' He held out his hand, ready to accept the dead bird.

Shrike met Corus' gaze. 'That's not how it works, Corus. You know that. You have to do it yourself. That's the whole point of the trial.'

Corus frowned. 'It'll be dark soon. There's no time. And besides, you know I can do it. Both of you. You know if I had a little longer I'd catch one of the creatures for myself. I almost had it...'

Shrike looked to Kadus, searching for support. 'I don't see what harm it can do,' said Kadus. 'He's right – if he had a little longer, he'd do it himself. Give it to him. That way, we can all leave together in the morning.'

Shrike felt a tightening in his chest. Something about this was wrong. The bird hadn't chosen Corus. It had chosen *him.* Yet he already had a bird of his own. Should he just leave the thing here to rot, along with his friend? It seemed like an unconscionable waste. What was to stop Corus claiming the bird as his own, regardless, after Shrike had discarded it? If he raised any objections back at the village, he might jeopardise his own position. Besides, Kadus had a point – there was no question in Shrike's mind that Corus would make a worthy Space Marine. What could it matter if Shrike gave him a little help over the finishing line now?

'Go on,' said Kadus. 'Hand it to him, and then we can get back before dark.'

'If you're sure,' said Shrike.

'You worry too much, Kayvaan,' said Kadus. 'It'll be fine. No one will ever know.'

I'll know, thought Shrike. He held out his hand and allowed Corus to scoop up the bird. He squirreled it away quickly in his pouch before Shrike could change his mind.

'Come on,' said Kadus, slapping him on the shoulder. 'It grows late, and Cordae awaits us.'

'Our *future* awaits us,' said Shrike.

'Together,' said Corus. 'The three of us. I shall not forget this, Shrike.'

Shrike had a sense that he, too, would remember that moment forever. He hoped he would never have cause to regret it.

'Do you ever look back, Kadus, and consider your life? All the choices you've made? Do you ever question what it might have been like if you had walked a different path?'

The Chapter Master stood in the gallery at the tip of the Ravenspire, staring up at the heavens. The light of distant Kiavahr cast a silvery pall across his face, bright and gibbous. The planet was a pale disc, mottled with brush-strokes of livid green – the great landmasses, near subsumed by the ever-living forest. The lights of sprawling cities winked in the darkness.

The sight of it filled him with longing. This was his home. To Shrike, it represented all that was pure and right – a planet blessed by the Emperor Himself, and touched by Corax, the greatest of warriors to ever know himself as Raven Guard.

Now, Shrike presided over all of it: Kiavahr, the Ravenspire, the Chapter. He had lived a long and blessed life of service to the Emperor, and carried the scars. The tau had recently felt his wrath in the Damocles Gulf; they would feel it again, soon enough.

Yet there was a single hint of regret, an error of judgement all those centuries ago, which still haunted him. A decision taken in haste that could not be undone, and yet had transpired to be an undoing. He thought of it, from time to time, particularly when he was here, on Deliverance, staring up at the ghostly light of his home world.

'You remember Corus,' said Kadus. 'You still punish yourself for his errors.'

'I punish myself for his death,' said Shrike. 'It is a different thing.'

'It was a long time ago. So many others have perished since then, and so many Raven Guard have been chosen in the cradle of the forest and forged in war.'

Shrike nodded, but did not turn to face his old friend. 'Yet it does not change the mistake we made,' said Shrike. 'Corus wasn't ready. I recognised it then, as I recognise it now. I was too proud and unsure of myself to speak up.'

'I pushed you to do it,' said Kadus. 'It was my decision.'

'It was *not*,' said Shrike, balling his hand into a fist. He wheeled on Kadus, not angry, but impassioned. 'I know my own mind, Kadus. I always have. I made the decision. You merely advised.'

'As I advise you now,' said Kadus. 'We must lay his spirit to rest. Both of us.'

Shrike opened his fist to reveal a tiny bird skull, yellowed and brittle with age. It had once belonged to Corus, given to Shrike all those years earlier, on Shenkar. 'Aye. That we must. And we shall do it in battle, smiting our enemies – not here, wallowing in the mistakes of the past. Too long have I concerned myself with what *might* have been. I must lay Corus to rest.'

'Gorkrusha,' said Kadus.

'Gorkrusha,' echoed Shrike. 'To this day he remains at large, spreading his filth and destruction across worlds. He has been a thorn in the side of the Imperium for too long. No longer can this continue. No longer will he be tolerated.'

'And you do this in the name of the Imperium, and not in the name of Corus?' said Kadus.

'I do this in the name of the Raven Guard,' said Shrike, 'and Corax.' He turned back to the window, his face cast half in shadow and half in planet-light. 'We shall not tolerate our enemies to live. Gorkrusha has been allowed to run rampant for too long. Now we will bring an end to his rampage.'

'You're going to hunt him?' said Kadus.

'No,' said Shrike. 'I've already found him.'

They gathered in the Eyrie, at the heart of their complex on Deliverance – the tallest tower on the moon, which burst through the cloud cover to afford a panoramic view of the stars, and of Kiavahr, far above, its surface awash with the amber light of the nearest sun.

Above their heads, in the upper reaches of the tower, ravens flocked, swooping low, hopping from rafter to rafter, chittering nervously as the Space Marines took their places around the table.

Drapes carrying the Chapter symbol of the Raven Guard hung from the stone walls, so low they brushed the floor, stirring with the motion of the warriors' passing.

The table was not a large one, but those who sat around it were amongst the finest warriors Shrike had ever known. To his left was Phaeros, now shadow captain of the Third Company, and beside him Cavaan, trusted veteran of Shrike's command squad. Arimdae was here, too, along with Kadus, Vaal and Solus. To Shrike's right sat Shadow Captain Koryn of the Fourth Company, veteran of Phideus XV, the Hroth campaign and the Sargassion Reach, resplendent in his ancient, engraved armour. Accompanying him were Argis and Grayvus, and Cordae, the Chaplain who had long ago passed Shrike through his initiation into the ranks of the Raven Guard. To this day, he had never seen the Chaplain's face beneath the sinister bird-skull mask, but he did not doubt his brother's integrity.

'Tell us, Brother Phaeros, what you have found,' said Shrike.

Phaeros stood. 'Some time ago, Master Shrike charged me with discovering the whereabouts of the ork warlord known as Gorkrusha.' Phaeros summoned a series of hololiths from the surface of the table before them.

'We found evidence of his campaigns in the Carpathion system, in which he had destroyed a moon, using sonic agitators to align the fragments into a resemblance of his famous glyph.' He enlarged one of the hololiths, and Shrike balked at the destruction and egoism on display.

Phaeros swiped away the hololiths, enlarging another. 'Then here, in the Hamuurian Cluster,' he said. The hololith showed a planet wrapped in ammonia ice, upon which Gorkrusha had melted the ice caps, burning his glyph into a continent-sized glacier. 'The melting of the ice caps released noxious fumes that poisoned the entire population.'

Phaeros pointed to a third image. 'Finally, we were able to follow his trail to this...' he hesitated, '*structure* in the Dalrinthian Arm.'

'What is it?' said Koryn, studying the hololith.

'A planet, of sorts,' said Shrike. 'He's manufactured

a small moon. The core is built from asteroids, lashed together to form a relatively stable base. As far as we can ascertain from the long-range picts, he's built structures across the surface of these asteroids, and used atmospheric generators to terraform its surface, giving it the semblance of a real, life-sustaining planet.'

'But what of these jagged formations,' asked Grayvus. 'What are those?'

'Shields,' said Phaeros. 'Immense impact shields erected at the poles. Each one is formed from a tectonic plate, gouged from another sundered world and emblazoned with the glyph. A "war world".'

'The power involved in such a feat is undeniable,' said Cordae. His head dipped as he spoke, his voice quiet, almost passive. 'This is no small thing you ask of us, master.'

It was not a criticism, Shrike knew. The Chaplain was ensuring that everyone around the table was aware of the inherent risks, Shrike included. In going after Gorkrusha, Shrike would be committing two entire companies of the Raven Guard to a war he might well lose.

'You wish to mount an invasion?' said Koryn.

Shrike pushed his chair back. A servitor scuttled out of his way, careful not to extinguish the candle it carried upon its back. 'I do,' he said, after a moment. 'For centuries that creature has plagued the Imperium. I've watched it slaughter millions of the Emperor's subjects, only to walk away, laughing, while their corpses burned. I can no longer tolerate its continued existence. We do the Imperium a great service by ending its campaign of destruction.'

'And yet I sense there is more to this, master, than mere duty,' said Cordae.

Shrike looked to the Chaplain, and saw only the empty sockets of the ancient roc staring back at him. He remembered that hollow stare from his days as an initiate on Kiavahr. He could not lie to it then, just as he could not lie to it now. Perhaps, he realised, that was why he had requested the Chaplain's presence here, today – because he knew that Cordae would not be swayed by talk of duty. He would seek the truth. When the Chaplain looked at him, he could not help but be reminded of the bird he had killed in the forest that fateful day; the way he had connected with it, how it had chosen *him*.

'You shall have the truth,' said Shrike, 'for I would not order you into battle in ignorance.' He walked slowly around the table, eyeing each of them in turn. 'I have fought the beast twice, and in both instances failed to kill it. In the process, I have lost brothers whom I have sworn to avenge. For me, this is a matter of honour, as well as duty. I will not go to the grave knowing that creature has outlived me, and without paying due respect to those we have lost in pursuit of it.'

Cordae nodded, his skull mask bobbing in bizarre mimicry of the bird it had once belonged to.

'Then we do this for duty, *and* for honour,' said Phaeros.

'Aye,' said Koryn. 'Let us show this greenskin the fist of the Imperium.'

'He'll be waiting for us,' said Kadus, who had remained silent throughout the briefing. 'Those are more than simple shields he's erected. He wanted to be found. He's taunting us, calling us out. That war world is not an attempt to build a planet – it's a stage. He's built it so we'll come.'

'Then come we shall,' said Shrike, 'and he shall feel our wrath.' He slammed his fist upon the table. 'Muster your troops, assemble your squadrons and sharpen your blades. We leave at dawn.'

Shrike turned his back as they rose from their seats, filing out of the room in silence. When he looked back, only Kadus remained, framed in the doorway. 'Now we put this matter to rest,' he said, with a sad smile.

'Aye,' said Shrike. 'It is time. For Corus.'

At Shrike's command, the Raven Guard's flotilla fell upon the war world with the might of the Emperor Himself. Three strike cruisers, armed with strafing las-cannons and payloads of super-heated plasma, began the bombardment, hanging in low orbit, scouring the planet's surface in preparation for the main Space Marine force. Within moments, the entire world was alight with gaudy streamers of plasma and flame.

Beneath them, thirty Thunderhawk gunships dived in neat formation, bursting through the thin atmos-phere, heavy bolters chattering as they ripped into the ork forces amassed below. Scores of Stormravens and Stormtalons swept low in their wake, engaging ork bombers and hammering ground troops with wave after wave of detonating shells.

From the deck of his battle-barge, Shrike watched his squadrons dive, saw the surface of the manufactured world blaze with the fires of war. In the distance hung the Stormtalon squadrons he was holding in reserve, waiting for the right moment to strike. From here, the vessels were nothing but scattered motes, barely visible against the black wash of space.

Anti-aircraft fire spat from scattered emplacements below, causing Stormtalons to bloom in the frigid void. Thunderhawks homed in on their fire, picking them off, causing their ammo dumps to explode in spectacular pillars of flame.

Soon, drop pods would fall like scattered seeds of death, tumbling into the midst of the greenskin forces and unfurling to reveal a hundred ebon-clad warriors.

Shrike's strategy was simple: the Third Company, led by Phaeros, would make planetfall in the inhabited region of the makeshift planet, accompanied by Shrike and his command squad, while Koryn's Fourth Company would maintain aerial cover, bombarding the orks from above and clearing a path for those on the ground – in particular, for Shrike and his command squad, as they searched for Gorkrusha.

Shrike stared down at the planet and watched its surface burn. This world was a monument to

Gorkrusha's vanity, nothing more. His looming, grinning glyph stared up at Shrike, seared into the craggy
face of his continental shields. He felt the call of it,
the taunt, and clenched his fists. The Raven's Claws
gleamed in the reflected starlight, sharp and ready.
Gorkrusha knew he was coming.

Shrike felt the battle-barge shudder, its engines
rumbling as it thundered towards the planet. Through
the viewing port, he watched more squadrons of
Thunderhawks fall away from their lines, dipping
down towards the surface, weapons blazing.

The speckled light of tracer fire burst from a
hundred or more locations on the surface in retaliation, from more emplacements, hidden amongst
ramshackle buildings and roads. Thunderhawks
detonated, opening like silent, flaming petals in the
void, before extinguishing just as swiftly, their debris
drifting gently in the airless vacuum.

The orks were clearly prepared, but this time,
Shrike knew, it would not be enough.

Slowly, inexorably, the battle-barge slid closer to
the planet, remaining just out of reach of enemy fire.

Shrike turned and marched towards the lower
decks, where servitors hurried about in orderly fashion, preparing for the drop assault.

He stalked to his own drop pod at the far end of
the launch bay, and stepped inside to find the rest
of his command squad already in position, clamped
within the narrow confines of the vehicle.

'Well met, brothers,' he said, as he ducked beneath

an overhanging brace and fastened himself into the waiting plasteel cocoon. The webbing slithered across his chest-plate, pinning him into place. He had never enjoyed the sensation of being trapped within such a confined space, although he relished what was to come. The drop pod would punch through the thin atmosphere, slamming them into the midst of combat, and Shrike would unleash the Raven's Claws. For once, the Raven Guard would not take to the shadows, but would come raging from the sky, spoiling for a fight.

The hatch shut with a pneumatic hiss, sealing them inside.

The mechanical voice of a servitor blared over the vox. 'Despatch in five, four, three, two...' The final digit was lost in the shudder of void-doors hinging open, and the pod's engines igniting with a kick.

Shrike watched through the tiny viewing port as the stars surged by, the pod falling from the barge like a dropped stone. Las-fire, tracer rounds and exploding Thunderhawks flashed by as the pod rolled, twisting towards its destination. He saw ork ships engaging the Stormtalons in low orbit, locked in combat as they ducked and weaved, each attempting to avoid the other's deadly fire.

Gyroscopic stabilisers whirred and alarms trilled as the drop pod struck the planet's atmosphere, flames caressing its heat shield and licking at the viewing port, casting everything beyond in a warm, orange glow.

Below, other pods thundered into the rocky ground like falling hammers, sending waves of orks sprawling, smearing their green corpses across the earth. Five enormous ork war machines stomped across the landscape, harried by Stormtalons that ducked and weaved, weapons barking as they pummelled thick armour plating, searching for any weak spots to exploit.

The orks formed a seething mass at the foot of these giants, thousands of them hooting and chanting as they fired up at the flashing vehicles above them, or hunkering down as Space Marines began to emerge from their fallen drop pods, shredding the xenos ranks with bolter fire. The fighting stretched for miles in all directions, an ocean of green, punctuated by pockets of black death.

The webbing tightened across Shrike's chest as the cradle shuddered and the pod was shunted sideways, either by a patch of extreme turbulence, or a glancing hit from one of the ork weapons. Undeterred, it continued its descent, now breaching the cloud cover and trailing coils of black smoke as its main engines guttered and cut out.

Kadus stood steadfast and silent in his own cradle, his expression hidden behind the faceplate of his helm. Beside him was Vaal, his head bowed, quietly chanting the Chapter's litanies to himself.

The pod struck earth, slamming into the rocky surface of the artificial world with a defiant crunch. It rebounded, alarms blaring as the hull was breached, three panels buckling under the force of the impact. It came down again a moment later, grinding noisily across the rocks, struggling to find purchase, until it finally came to rest a few seconds later, wedged against a jagged outcropping.

Shrike sliced open his webbing and hauled himself free from his cradle, swinging under the brace. He could hear the thunderous pounding of other drop pods landing outside, heralds of death from above.

There was a chime from around the other side of the pod, and the walls around Shrike began to shake as they tried to peel open. 'Only one of the hatches is working,' said Arimdae. 'We'll have to exit the pod from aro–' His words were cut short by the boom of a weapon firing at close proximity. The shot echoed inside the pod, a sharp, percussive bang. The stench of smoke and boiling blood filled the air.

Arimdae burbled for a moment over the vox, and then fell silent. Cavaan, already free of his webbing, tore his bolt pistol from its holster and let loose at whatever it was that had ended his battle-brother's life.

Shrike scrambled to get around to the open hatch. He found Cavaan standing in the opening, three dead orks slumped by his feet. Dark blood had spattered his armour, as he'd burst their skull cavities at point-blank range.

Arimdae had been thrown back into his cradle by the force of the shot, a fist-sized hole in his chest. It was clear the life had gone out of him immediately;

his body was folded awkwardly, his limbs hanging limp and lifeless. Blood covered the wall behind him, and scorch marks stained the metalwork where he'd been standing.

'Fetch his corvia, Vaal,' said Shrike. There was no time for sentimentality; there was work to be done. Arimdae would be mourned later.

Shrike stepped out onto the rocky surface, snapping the bones of the dead orks underfoot as he trod on them. Drop pods were still streaming out of the sky in their multitudes, their smoky trails like scars across the pale blue canopy. Overhead, Thunderhawks swept by, their engines rending the air, their weapons shredding anything in their path. He could see nothing but the battle, stretching away into the distance, lighting up this parody of a planet.

Around him, the Third Company had deployed in all its glory, and ebon-armoured warriors burst from their drop pods in a hail of bolter fire, cutting down any and all orks who awaited them.

Shrike took four of the creatures with shots to the back of their heads, dropping them where they stood. Behind him, the rest of his command squad were emerging from the ruins of their drop pod, engaging the enemy.

There were orks everywhere, and the air was filled with the thunder of weapons fire. The ground beside Shrike erupted as stubber fire from above chewed the rocky earth, and he fired his bolt pistol, punching holes in a low-flying ork aircraft as it swung around, preparing to make another pass.

Before Shrike could squeeze off another burst, the aircraft exploded in a ball of flame and a black Stormtalon swooped past, already searching for its next target.

The rumble of the ork war machines caused the ground to shake. These things were serving as a rallying point for the ork infantry, and now that the Space Marine ground troops had deployed, the Thunderhawks had begun to concentrate their fire on them, pounding them with heavy bolter fire.

Shrike powered his jump pack and barrelled into a wall of orks, his Raven's Claws flashing, their heads rolling from their shoulders in a shower of ichor. He speared another through the gut, a second through the chest, a third in the shoulder, rending its arm from its torso. His armour dripped in gore as he cut a swathe through the green tide, his blood singing in his veins. He lost count of the numbers that fell in his wake; it was enough to know that they were dead.

Around him, his command squad formed a circle, pushing back the orks, heaps of greenskin corpses twitching as they carved a path towards a nearby rocky promontory.

Shrike twisted, felling two orks at once, spilling their intestines over their boots, even as their axes scored his armour. He boosted towards the promontory, his talons carving the face of another ork as he lifted into the air.

He came down beside Kadus, who was firing into the mass of orks before him, dropping them before they'd even had a chance to raise their weapons and take aim.

Shrike searched the horizon. In the distance there were buildings, giving the impression of a ramshackle city, although Shrike suspected it was, in truth, simply a collection of rough bunkers and ammunition dumps.

They'd been unable to map the bizarre structure remotely, but Shrike knew that finding Gorkrusha would be a simple matter. He would make haste to the biggest, grandest structure on the war world, and he was certain to find the ork lurking there. He had a sense, he believed, of how the orks' primitive minds worked – always searching for self-aggrandisement, always aiming to prove their dominance over others of their species. Shrike would use this to his advantage, he decided, if he were able to get close enough to the beast.

He glanced around as Amrike opened fire on another ork who'd strayed too close, and it fell back, gurgling and clutching at its throat. A squad of nearby orks scattered as Kadus dropped one of them, only to stumble into the sights of a Stormtalon, which swooped low, ripping them apart with its thundering autocannons.

The orks here didn't appear to be organised, at least not in the way that Shrike had expected. There was no sense of Gorkrusha's presence.

'This isn't where the fight is,' he said, looking to Kadus.

'There are thousands of them here,' said Vaal, confused by Shrike's words.

'And look how easily we're taking them apart,' said Shrike. 'These creatures are nothing but sacrificial pawns in Gorkrusha's greater game. They lack direction. They're here as fodder.'

'Then lead us to the fight,' said Kadus. 'Phaeros and Koryn can finish what we've started here. Show us the way.'

'I intend to,' said Shrike. He pointed to the haphazard collection of buildings on the horizon. 'We start *there*.'

As Shrike reached the city, he was suddenly back on Shenkar.

He dropped low, soaring through the familiar streets on a plume of flame, his jump pack roaring. The buildings here were nothing but a parody of the Imperial cities that Gorkrusha had spent so many years destroying, empty shells erected to mimic hab-blocks and manufactorums, but it was more than that; the layout was familiar, too.

'I recognise this place,' said Kadus, over the vox. 'I've been here before.'

'It's Shenkar,' said Cavaan. 'He's recreated it here.' The incredulity was evident in his voice.

'He's dressing the stage for our final confrontation,' said Shrike. If the ork's intention was to undermine his confidence, it had already failed; the ploy had succeeded only in strengthening his resolve.

Shrike cut the power to his jump pack, dropping to the ground. The others fell in behind him. 'We're close to the centre now,' he said. 'The plaza in Shenkar where we landed when we first deployed. That's where we'll find him. That's where I will settle this debt.'

He set out at a run, ghosting through the familiar streets. The Raven Guard were not the only spectres in this place, Shrike considered. The dead of Shenkar – the fallen warriors of the Astra Militarum, dragged from their vehicles and put to death; the civilians murdered in their beds – were here too. He had vowed that day to avenge them, to ensure the orks paid for such grave losses with their own lives. Again, on Evenfall, the Imperium's death toll had numbered in the millions, and Shrike had once more taken that burden upon himself, that quest for vengeance.

The streets wound on through the false city, and the Space Marines followed, drawing closer to the heart of the complex with every step. They moved in silence, constantly on guard for any sign of skulking orks, but the streets had a stark air of abandonment, and Shrike had the impression that nothing living had passed through here for some time.

Behind them, the battle still raged, Koryn and Phaeros' forces laying waste to any hint of ork resistance. They'd cut a swathe through the green tide to allow Shrike and his squad clear passage – now they were engaged in bringing down the ork war machines. The inhabited regions of this place were small, and the ork forces were pinned. The Raven Guard would not pass up the opportunity to destroy them.

The sky was ablaze with flame, and the entire planet trembled beneath Shrike's boots, rocked by the constant churn of explosives. By the time the Raven Guard had finished, this lashed-up caricature of a planet would be nought but dust and rubble.

This, though, had never been about the orks. Shrike knew this with a sharpness of purpose that he had known only once before, back on Kiavahr, during those final hours of the hunt. It had always been about Gorkrusha.

The warlord was a uniter, a leader capable of instilling the orks with purpose. He brought direction to their need for wanton destruction, channelling it, turning it into something greater. In this way, he had slain worlds. It might have been an admirable quality in a human; in an ork it was a deadly threat. The Imperium had put down many such warlords in the past – Gorkrusha was long overdue extermination.

Up ahead, the street narrowed, the walls pressing in to form a channel that terminated in a massive gateway formed from beaten metal plates, and shaped to resemble Gorkrusha's glyph. The opening was twenty feet high, passing directly through the tusked maw of the beast.

'We're being channelled into a trap,' said Kadus.

'Not a trap,' said Shrike. 'A reckoning.'

'Then we should call in the Thunderhawks,' said Cavaan. 'If he's here, we can level the place and be done with it.'

'No,' said Shrike. 'This is not about levelling the place. I shall not rest until I have seen his corpse with my own eyes.'

'Then be on your guard,' said Kadus. 'He knows we're coming.'

'Stay here,' said Shrike. 'Whatever happens, wait until I give the word.' He looked to each of them in turn. 'Do you understand?'

He waited until they had all given their acknowledgement. Kadus caught his arm. 'For Corus,' he said.

'For Corus,' echoed Shrike.

He walked towards the gate and stepped through, onwards into the light.

There was a deafening roar and Shrike looked up to see row upon row of orks, gathered in the towers of the surrounding buildings, looking down at him and jeering.

He was in some sort of arena. The floor was comprised of more sheets of beaten metal, polished smooth and gleaming, and overhead, gaudy banners fluttered in the wind, hung from poles around the edges of the arena. Plumes of fire roared from enormous braziers, one at either side of a massive effigy of Gorkrusha, which had been constructed from the remains of Imperial vehicles, battered and fashioned into the shape of the warlord.

Gorkrusha himself sat upon an enormous throne at the far end of the arena. He'd aged since Shrike had last seen him on Evenfall; one of his tusks had grown rotten and broken, and an old wound ran from the bridge of his nose to his jaw, wrinkling his upper lip with puckered scar tissue. A new shoulder brace had been fashioned from thick sheet metal, adorned in black-and-white checks, and his exoskeleton had been upgraded, with larger pistons fitted to his thighs and calves. His feet had now been entirely replaced by mechanical claws.

The throne upon which he lounged had an odd, angular look, and as Shrike peered at it, he recognised first the shape of a vambrace, then a shoulder guard, decorated with the faded sigil of a Space Wolf. With disgust, he realised that the throne had been constructed from the power armour of dead Space Marines – Blood Angels, Space Wolves and Flesh Tearers amongst them – and Shrike could see evidence that the armour had not been entirely devoid of body parts when the seat was constructed. The skull of one unlucky battle-brother currently served as a footrest.

Shrike clenched his jaw, resisting the urge to rush at the beast.

Gorkrusha's familiar drill-fist whirred, taunting Shrike, and his single red eye glinted in the reflected sunlight as he turned his head, taking in his arena.

This was the final confirmation. This place – *this entire planet* – had been constructed for this single encounter. An arena designed to trap Shrike within it, to force him to commit his troops and take on Gorkrusha alone. The scale of it was incredible.

Slowly, the ork warlord rose from his seat, grinding the Space Marine's skull beneath his heel as he stood. Another roar went up from the orks gathered in the buildings above. There must have been hundreds of them, jostling for space at the windows, clambering on the roofs.

Gorkrusha lumbered forwards. He raised his drill-fist, pointing it at Shrike. 'Puny man-thing.' Its voice was a rumbling bellow that caused the human words to sound alien and wrong. 'How many times must I kill you, Space Marine?' He spat the final two words. 'This shall be the last.'

Shrike chose not to dignify the creature with an answer. He raised his Raven's Claws, folding them across his chest in a stance of readiness. They crackled and hummed with the rage of Corax himself, eager to shed ork blood.

Gorkrusha leapt from the throne, propelled forwards by the pistons in his legs. He came down fast and hard, nearly taking Shrike by surprise, but Shrike boosted deftly out of the way, and Gorkrusha's drill-fist bit into the ground, chewing up the burnished metal.

Gorkrusha laughed, righting himself in a spray of dust. Shrike jabbed forwards with his lightning claws. The ork lurched back, and the tips brushed his shoulder guard, scratching furrows in the paintwork.

'Faster, harder,' the beast growled, in broken Gothic. Shrike didn't know if it was intended as a compliment or a suggestion. He heard the crowd roar, baying for his blood, and realised that for Gorkrusha, this was as much about proving himself as revenge. All of these orks – they'd seen what the Raven Guard had done, bringing down his lair on Shenkar, burning thousands of their kin on Evenfall. This was about Gorkrusha cementing his rule, showing that he was worthy to lead these greenskins.

Shrike was about to prove that he was not.

Gorkrusha lurched forwards, swinging his other fist in a sweeping, downward arc. Shrike eluded the blow at the last moment, hoping the creature would overbalance itself, but Gorkrusha was far too clever for that, and turned the momentum into a spin. He wheeled on the spot, coming back at Shrike again, this time catching him fully in the chest with a round-house blow that lifted him from his feet.

Shrike felt the wind leave his lungs as his chest-plate buckled and cracked, coolant spraying from a disconnected hose. He launched into the air, his head snapping backwards, and sailed across the courtyard, slamming back down to the ground in a rough heap. He coughed, spitting blood inside his helm.

He heard thundering footsteps and activated his jump pack, shooting across the ground just as Gorkrusha's drill-fist came down again, splintering the paving slabs and burring angrily as it scraped across the rocky ground beneath.

Shrike cut the power to his jump pack, lurching to his feet.

Gorkrusha was breathing raggedly from the exertion as he pounded across the arena and swung again, extending his drill-fist as he threw himself bodily at Shrike, aiming to pin him to the wall.

Shrike twisted, flicking out his claws and raking them down Gorkrusha's torso as he leapt out of the way. The ork roared in fury, crashing heavily into the wall, its armour torn asunder and bright ribbons of flesh hanging from four long gouges in its chest.

Shrike circled it, claws glinting.

He saw the ork's next move before it came, but allowed it anyway, taking a piston-powered leg full in the shoulder. It cracked his pauldron and sent him sprawling to the ground. Pain flared, and the analgesics in his suit cut in, immediately dulling the sensation.

Above, the spectators cheered. Gorkrusha was laughing again as he dragged himself to his feet, wincing at the pain in his chest. Blood was dribbling down his torso, dripping down his legs, but it seemed only to slow him fractionally, as he stomped over to where Shrike was still laying on the ground, dragging himself slowly away from the encroaching ork.

Gorkrusha had the scent of blood now, and Shrike could see it in his remaining eye; he was moving in for the kill.

He stood over Shrike, drool dripping from his gargantuan jaws, glowering down at him with a look that almost resembled pity. 'Now, you die,' he said, raising his drill-fist above his head. He emitted a bellowing roar that sent the crowd wild. They were chanting something Shrike couldn't understand, something crude and orkish, but he gathered the meaning all too well. They were telling Gorkrusha to finish him.

Shrike had fought the beast twice, on Shenkar and on Evenfall, and on both occasions he had failed to kill it. He knew, in his heart, that he would not kill it here, either.

That was the difference between him and this creature – where Gorkrusha fought to prove his worth, to demonstrate his strength to his fellow greenskins, Shrike fought for a cause, for the Imperium of Man, for Corax, and his brothers fought alongside him. Theirs was not a life of personal gain, nor was it a life alone, like that of the vile creature who now stood over him, gloating – a creature that these other orks would just as soon see dead and buried so that one of them might take its place.

Shrike looked past Gorkrusha's leg to the gateway through which he had entered the arena. Gorkrusha had his back to it, fixated only on Shrike and delivering his killing blow.

'Corus,' said Shrike.

Gorkrusha paused, a quizzical expression on his face. He searched the Space Marine for any sense of meaning, but then his eye glazed over once again, and, shaking his head as if dismissing the Space

Marine's outburst, he thrust his drill-fist down towards Shrike's helm.

Shrike caught the ork's arm with both hands, straining against the immense strength of the creature, the screaming drill only inches from his faceplate.

The crowd roared again, screaming for Gorkrusha, and he laughed, clouded by arrogance and misunderstanding their warning.

Shrike could not beat this beast alone. But he wasn't alone.

'Now you di–' Gorkrusha never finished the sentence, as a chainsword punched through his chest from behind, splintering ribs and causing him to cry out in pain. He twisted, trying to shift his bulk, but another chainsword burst through his gut, rupturing organs and grinding against his metal exoskeleton.

Gorkrusha roared as a third, and then a fourth chainsword chewed into his torso, sawing through bones, rending his heart into shreds.

He froze, confused, and then the expression on his face altered, and Shrike lashed out to remove his head with a single swipe of his claws. It landed a few feet away, its lonely eye still watching Shrike, accusatory, lifeless.

Kadus gave the ork's body a shove and it toppled sideways, sprawling across the ground with a metallic thud. Blood gushed from multiple wounds, forming glossy pools around it on the paving stones. One of the mechanical legs spasmed, and then, finally, the drill bit ceased its constant burr, and everything fell still.

The crowd of orks in the upper storeys were going wild, scrabbling at one another as they tried to decide whether to attack the five Space Marines, or run for their lives.

Vaal reached down and proffered his hand, helping Shrike to his feet. 'What are we going to do about the rest of them?' he said.

Shrike reached up and unclipped his helm. He dragged at the thin air, pulling it down into his lungs. 'Watch the skies,' he said, grimly.

Within seconds, three squadrons of Stormtalons were swooping overhead, autocannons chattering as they sprayed the ork buildings with enough rounds to bring the entire edifice sliding to the ground. Any orks who weren't rent apart by the weapons fire were crushed by the collapsing structures, or trampled by other orks as they tried desperately to get away.

Shrike crossed to Gorkrusha's decapitated head, staring down at it, contemplative.

'You said you were going to kill it alone,' said Cavaan. It wasn't an accusation, but a question.

Shrike shook his head. 'I said that I would not rest until I saw its corpse,' he said. 'There is a difference.' He looked at Cavaan, but saw there was no understanding in his eyes. This had been Shrike's kill to make, his mission of vengeance. Why then had he allowed the others to finish it?

'We are nothing as individuals, Cavaan. It is only

our brotherhood that makes us strong. These orks do not understand that. They blindly follow those that are bigger, taller, more fearsome. They live by fear, and fear alone. Each of us, however – every single one of us – is part of something far greater.'

'Aye,' said Cavaan. 'We are Raven Guard.'

Shrike nodded.

In the distance, a series of explosions marked the detonation of an ork war machine. Koryn and Phaeros were still at work, mopping up the last of the greenskins.

A Stormraven was descending from above, ready to extract them.

He watched it land, the embarkation hatch hissing open. He had finished with Gorkrusha, but there was still one last thing to be done.

The forest was all. The forest was everything.

Shrike stood amongst the bolus trees, breathing deep of the forest. It was late afternoon, and the light was dying, a few last golden shafts brushing the boughs of the trees as the sun slipped below the distant horizon.

He'd removed his armour and now stood only in his ceremonial robes, his coal-black eyes scanning the gloaming. Kadus stood a short distance behind him, watching silently.

Shrike crossed the glade to the foot of the bolus tree, and then took two paces, out to where the fallen branch had once sat. He crouched, rummaging around in the red and gold leaves until he found the hollow he had made here, many moons ago. He slipped his hand into his pocket and withdrew the fragile little bird skull, dangling it before him on a silver chain so fine that it might have been a thread of hair.

Slowly, reverently, he placed the skull into the hollow, and used the edge of his hand to scoop over a small mound of earth, pressing it down so that it covered the corvia.

'Now it is done,' he said. His voice seemed to carry in the glade, startling the birds overhead. He thought perhaps they'd been watching him, too.

'Now we have made it right,' said Kadus.

Shrike rose to his feet. He sighed. 'No. Don't you see, Kadus? It was never *wrong*. I understand that now.'

Shrike crossed to Kadus and led him away from the glade. Their footsteps rustled amongst the crisp leaves. 'Cordae, he knew it, too,' he said. 'All along, he understood what had happened out here, in the forest, and still he let it pass. It was never our responsibility, never our decision to allow Corus to pass his initiation.'

'But he didn't pass,' said Kadus. 'We gave him that raven. You and I. Everything that came after that was our responsibility.'

'No,' said Shrike. 'That was the real test. The hunt was simply a tool. Cordae wasn't interested in whether or not we could catch a bird. He wanted to know how far we'd go to get one, and whether we would help one another. He was testing our bond, our sense of brotherhood. That is what makes us Raven Guard, Kadus. That is what defines us.'

'Then it was us who might have failed,' said Kadus, 'if we had not allowed Corus to come with us.'

'Precisely,' said Shrike. 'Corus made his mistakes, but they were *his* mistakes to make. He paid for them with his life.'

'And now we have honoured him, here on Kiavahr,' said Kadus, 'for a life well lived in the service of the Chapter.'

'Aye,' said Shrike. 'Now he is at peace.'

The light was almost gone now, the forest hushed and peaceful. Together, the two brothers walked to their transport and set a course home, for Deliverance.

ABOUT THE AUTHOR

George Mann is an author and editor
based in the East Midlands. For Black
Library, he is best-known for his stories
featuring the Raven Guard, which include
the anthology *Sons of Corax*, the audio
dramas *Helion Rain* and *Labyrinth of
Sorrows*, the novella *The Unkindness of
Ravens*, plus a number of short stories.

SPACE MARINE
LEGENDS

WARHAMMER
40,000

CASSIUS

BEN COUNTER

An extract from

CASSIUS

by Ben Counter

The engines screamed and the world called Kolovan screamed back, the howl of a toxic storm that roared and scraped at the lower hull of the drop pod. Cassius knew the violent sensations of a drop pod assault intimately: the chill wail of the thin upper atmosphere, the hammering of the retro jets firing up, the hiss and buffet as the pod punched down through cloud cover and the rising bellow of the jets fighting against the thickening air.

As the pod screeched into its final descent attitude, these sensations were as familiar as taking a breath. Leaning into the pod's lurches was like taking a step or speaking a word.

'Clear your minds, brethren,' said Cassius, trusting in the amplified vox-channel to carry his voice above the storm of the descent. 'Seize upon only that symbol that shall lead you to victory. The sacrifice of Lord Guilliman. A passage from the Codex. The sight of blessed Macragge from space. An emblem of all we fight for. Take it and focus on it, and your soul shall be ready for the fight. Be pure and steel-hearted! Be all that is fury and righteousness!'

He was making his descent to the surface alongside a Tactical squad from the Third Company. Sergeant Verigar led them, a grey-haired veteran whose temple and left cheek glinted with the dull sheen of bionics. For now his stern visage was hidden beneath the pitiless iron mask of his red Mark VII helmet, and he sat with the easy calm of a warrior who had been through dozens, hundreds, of landings like this. Cassius had not fought beside Verigar before, but Captain Fabian spoke highly of him. He knew the names and faces of the others, but had not yet ascribed particular value to any of them. He would see them fight, and then he would know them.

The grav-restraints tightened and forced Cassius back into the plasteel frame holding his armoured body in place. A moment later the drop pod slammed into the ground. The retro engines and shock absorbers did not completely cancel out the teeth-rattling impact, and Cassius' head snapped back and forth with the force.

The restraint around Cassius' right arm snapped free. The Chaplain drew his crozius arcanum from its compartment at his side.

He was armed. He was ready to kill.

The explosive bolts in the drop pod's upper hull fired like a series of gunshots. Light blared in as the hull split into four sections and fell away, exposing the Space Marines inside to the sun of Kolovan for the first time.

The star that hovered overhead and shone between clouds of filthy brown toxins was a painful, acid yellow. It fell on a broken plain, as if the surface had been baked hard by that sun and then shattered by a vast hammer. Deep fissures broke the land up into patches of scorched ground, and fingers of pale rock broke through, the bones of the planet, where the ground had been particularly tortured. A distant line of smouldering mountains spoke of the geological activity that had torn this place up over and over again.

More drop pods bearing the colours of the Third and Fifth Companies were thudding home, raising splintering showers of broken earth. As the crafts' bolts fired, squads of Ultramarines leapt out, weapons raised and ready to kill, the blue of their armour discoloured by the sickly filter of Kolovan's sun.

Cassius' grav-restraints snapped open, and he jumped from the drop pod as his men disembarked alongside him. A thousand battles' worth of experience flooded through him and he took a tally of the landscape around him in the space of a few seconds.

Broken ground, difficult to move over swiftly. Rises and breaks in the earth could serve as cover. The rest of the strike force was making landfall closely-grouped, for the crew of the ship *Defence of Talassar* had performed their task well in launching the drop pods from upper orbit.

The air was toxic. It would have dropped a normal man in a couple of minutes. A Space Marine's constitution could survive it initially but it would build up over time, and so Cassius wore a rebreather unit over his mouth and nose. The toxins stung the skin that still remained on his blasted face, the wind that carried them sharp with the dirt whipped up by the drop pod's impact.

'*We're east of the drop zone!*' came a vox on the command channel from Captain Galenus of the Fifth Company. '*The xenos are massing from the south.*'

'*Sigillite's teeth,*' swore Captain Fabian of the Third over the vox. '*We expected no resistance here.*'

'Do I detect dismay, brother-captain?' said Cassius. 'This is but a drop in the ocean compared to what will come. Let the men test their fury. It will do them good.'

Cassius turned to the battle-brothers emerging from the drop pod. 'The tyranids were not so distant as we feared,' he said. 'They mass and respond from the south. We take the southern ridge, and we hold it until our main force makes landfall.'

His squad nodded gravely. Gauntleted fingers rested on weapon studs. Blades were checked and stowed. They were ready.

'We hold the ridge,' Cassius repeated through the vox. 'Fabian, you are with me. Captain Galenus, take position to the east and be wary of flanking attacks. Let them come in their thousands, and let them feel the wrath of Guilliman's sons. We are the wall against which the enemy will break.'

'Move out,' growled Sergeant Verigar, wisely leaving the oratory to his Chaplain.

'Let us send the foul xenos shrieking into the abyss,' roared Brother Ortius, doing the opposite.

Cassius let it pass. He knew what strength the expression of battle-joy gave them, and he knew what it covered up. Like everything else, it was there to be used by leaders like Cassius, turned into another weapon in the arsenal of the Ultramarines.

Other squads from Third Company joined with his own, while the landing forces of the Fifth secured the eastern edge of the ridge – Tactical squads, standing tall and proud in their burnished warplate, ready to face the enemy with a torrent of bolter fire; Assault Marines, chainswords already roaring with eager fury; and Devastator squads wielding pristine plasma cannons, missile launchers and heavy flamers. The latter would be key, Cassius knew; disciplined bolter drill and skilful bladework had their place in any battle, but against the swirling, writhing horror of a tyranid swarm, a swathe of cleansing flame or a sanctified warhead engraved with holy rites and packed with refined explosives were often the more effective countermeasures.

Cassius ran up the ridge of broken earth to the south of the drop pod site. As he crested it he saw the land reached down into a shallow depression where once an ancient river had fed a lake now long-drained by the land's upheaval. Into that bowl flowed not water but a mass of chittering, scrabbling flesh, a thousand limbs, the acidic sun gleaming on glossy carapaces and glinting on rows of sharp teeth.

Tyranid battle-organisms, numbering in the hundreds. They were termagants and hormagaunts, creatures evolved to serve as the foot soldiers of the hive mind, to swarm in massive numbers and flood the battlefield with gnashing teeth. Towering over them were a dozen warrior-forms that stalked on their two hind legs and lashed at the smaller creatures with whips of living flesh. The tyranids of each hive fleet had their own appearance and colouration, and these specimens had a particularly ill look to them – maggot-pale skin and plates of ivory exoskeletal armour, with eyes as black as night and maws full of glinting white teeth.

There were two options. The first was to wait at the ridge for the tyranids to reach the Ultramarines, withering their numbers with bolter fire. The second was to advance to meet them and fight them face to face, driving a wedge of power-armoured fury into the heart of the aliens.